Joana
Scott

6/4/99

A Will to Kill

JOHN PENN

A Will to Kill

CHARLES SCRIBNER'S SONS   NEW YORK

First published in the United States by Charles Scribner's Sons 1984

Copyright © 1983 John Penn

Library of Congress Cataloging in Publication Data

Penn, John.
A will to kill.

I. Title.
PR6066.E496W5   1984   823'.914   84-1410
ISBN 0-684-18174-6

1 3 5 7 9 11 13 15 17 19 H/C 20 18 16 14 12 10 8 6 4 2

Printed in the United States of America.

A Will to Kill

CHAPTER 1

English weather was, for once, a justified subject of conversation that August. Dry, clear days of bright sunshine and moderate temperatures alternated with periods of growing heat and humidity, culminating in scattered but massive electrical storms. Even a small tornado had been reported in the south-west. As usual the weather men maintained that such conditions were not really so extraordinary, but people at large talked of one of the most trying summers in living memory.

This Monday was particularly uncomfortable in the Cotswolds — hot and sultry, with thunder circling the area of the small market town of Colombury promising relief but not bringing it. It was the sort of weather in which tempers frayed easily, and Peter Derwent's temper was very badly frayed.

Standing in the middle of Trevor Grayson's sitting-room, fists clenched, arms rigid at his sides, Derwent glared at his host, who rose slowly and calmly from the depths of an armchair to face his uninvited guest. Grayson was half a head shorter and ten years older than Derwent, but most men would have backed him in a fight. He would certainly have backed himself.

Not that he had any desire to fight Peter Derwent. On the contrary, as he looked at the tall, slope-shouldered figure standing stubbornly before him and noted the lines in the long, narrow face and the hair already greying at the sides, Grayson felt something akin to affection for his neighbour.

But his irritation was equally real. He'd been having a lazy afternoon, watching with a vague sense of impropriety one of those football matches that these days seemed to appear on television even in the middle of summer, when he'd seen Derwent approaching across the lawn. He hadn't really welcomed the interruption. The weather was getting to him, and that extra pint of beer at lunch had been a mistake. Then Derwent had surprised him, and started being bloody importunate. He'd felt the muscles tighten at the back of his neck and he'd promptly laughed in Derwent's face.

'And that's positively your last word?' Peter Derwent said, containing his anger with obvious difficulty.

'Positively. I'm sorry. But as I told you I can't afford—'

'You can't afford! You—'

Whatever uncomplimentary, even vicious, remark Derwent intended to add was cut short by a vivid flash of lightning that lit up the whole of Trevor Grayson's sitting-room, momentarily highlighting the Stubbs over the mantel, the sporting prints on the opposite wall, the expensive modern furniture and the room's general air of quiet opulence. It was followed almost immediately by a clap of thunder, so loud and violent that the house seemed to shake on its foundations, as if a heavy bomb had exploded nearby. Then, as the reverberations receded, the rain suddenly came sheeting down.

Grayson ran to shut the windows. Derwent made no effort to help, but just stood and watched. He had been so absorbed in his argument with Grayson—if their ludicrous conversation could be called an argument—that he hadn't noticed the dark thunderheads gathering in the sky or the growing gloom in the house. Though, like everyone else in and around Colombury, he'd been expecting the storm to break all day, the sudden violence of the weather had taken him by surprise and somehow drained away his anger, leaving him spent and resigned.

'I'd better be going,' he said. 'It's clear you won't change your mind. Silly of me to think you would, but—'

There was a tap at the door and a small, fat, wellcorseted woman came into the room. 'Excuse me, sir,' said Mrs Wilson, Grayson's housekeeper. 'I just wanted to make sure everything was all right in here. I've checked the rest of the downstairs. I shut up the top floor earlier when I saw the storm coming.'

'Good.' Grayson's square, hard face broke into a smile of approval. 'Everything's fine here, Mrs Wilson, but an early cup of tea wouldn't go amiss.'

'Not for me,' Derwent said at once. 'I told you I was off.'

'But not in this, Mr Derwent!' Mrs Wilson exclaimed. 'You'll be wet through before you've gone ten yards. Look! It's fair pelting down. And I wouldn't trust this storm. It's a bad one, and there's a lot of thunder and lightning close at hand.'

She looked anxiously from Peter Derwent to her employer. She had been tidying the dining-room, across the hall from the sitting-room, and she'd heard their raised voices. Mr Derwent had been shouting. And that wasn't like him; he was normally such a kind and considerate man. So something Mr Grayson had done or refused to do must have annoyed him very much. Admittedly she'd listened, but she hadn't caught more than the odd word: the row seemed to be somehow connected with money and land. Anyway, it wasn't her business.

'Tea's just what we need, Mrs Wilson. And of course Mr Derwent will stay,' Grayson said firmly. 'Even if you're prepared to brave the weather, Peter, you can't turn down an offer of some of Mrs Wilson's homemade scones.'

'I'm afraid I must.' Derwent's voice was tight as he moved purposefully towards the sitting-room door. 'I have to get home. I've work to do.'

'Well, if you won't wait, you won't. But at least you must borrow a raincoat.' Solicitous, Grayson followed Derwent into the hall. 'Otherwise you'll get soaked to the skin, and we can't have you catching your death of cold, Peter. That would never do.' Grayson laughed as if at some private joke.

'If you're sure, Mr Derwent . . .' Mrs Wilson glanced from one man to the other, sensing the continuing tension between them. 'I think Mr Grayson's oilskin would be best.'

'That's it. My old yellow slicker. That'll keep you dry if anything will.'

Peter Derwent was clearly reluctant to accept any favour, but he realized the stupidity of going out into the storm unprotected. He watched while Mrs Wilson went to the hall cupboard and produced a yellow oilskin with an attached hood. 'Thanks,' he said as she helped him into it. 'I'll get one of the children to return it tomorrow.'

'No hurry.'

Trevor Grayson opened the front door and involuntarily took a step backwards as a flurry of rain and leaves blew into the house. The really torrential downpour had ceased, but it was still raining hard and thunder was growling ominously in the distance. Suddenly, as they stood by the open door, the black clouds above them were split by a jagged line of lightning.

'Sure you won't change your mind, Peter?'

Derwent didn't hesitate. 'I'm sure. Goodbye.'

Grayson shut the front door almost before Peter Derwent was clear of the step, and paused, his back against it. He shook his head as if puzzled by Derwent's insistence on leaving, and grinned ruefully. Really he was considering whether he should offer Mrs Wilson some explanation for the raised voices he was sure she must have heard earlier. He decided against it; explanations would only serve to impress the incident on her mind, and he didn't want to start any gossip if it could be avoided.

Instead he said, 'What a day! I'd rather Mr Derwent was out in it than me. But I think I'd still like that early tea, Mrs Wilson.' With a casual nod he went back into his sitting-room.

Head down, Peter Derwent strode down the short gravelled drive. He didn't mind the weather. To some extent he got a grim satisfaction from it. The darkening sky, occasionally split with lightning, the murmur of thunder, the steady mournful rain that from time to time was blown in gusts across his face — all this matched his mood. Damn Grayson, he thought. Why, for once, couldn't Grayson have helped? Couldn't afford it, indeed! Reaching the road, Derwent stared resentfully back at the beautiful honey-coloured cottage that Trevor Grayson now owned.

It had originally been built by Peter Derwent's father, Gerald, for his sister Nina after she had been widowed during the Second World War. But Peter's Aunt Nina had never lived there. By the time she returned to Oxfordshire Gerald's wife had died, and Nina came to live with her brother in the big house, Broadfields, that had belonged to the Derwents for over a hundred and fifty years. She had helped to bring up Gerald's two small sons, Michael the elder who had later died abroad, and Peter himself. She still lived at Broadfields, now with Peter and his own family. As for the cottage, it had been sold and resold, to be bought some four and a half years ago by Grayson, who had known Michael in Africa.

The acre of land on which the cottage stood had been carved out of the Derwents' property, but Broadfields house was some twenty minutes away by road. Cutting through the Derwents' woods could halve the distance and Peter Derwent, his mind pondering his personal problems, automatically turned off the road, sloshed his way across a narrow ditch and took a path through the trees.

The ancient Cotswold town of Colombury had been

growing steadily for some years, and by now development had spread past the Grey Dove, the pub at the Y-junction that marked the southern end of the Derwent property. Along the left-hand fork beyond the pub the local authority had built a row of council houses almost opposite Grayson's cottage and the main entrance to Broadfields. The right-hand fork led past the old Norman church of St Mary the Virgin and the rectory beside it. Apart from the church, its equally ancient churchyard and the rectory, Grayson's cottage and the pub, Peter Derwent's estate included all the land within the arms of the 'Y' formed by the two forking roads.

The path that Peter Derwent was taking was one of several that crossed his land, and it was frequently used by local people. Questions of right of way had never arisen; over the years this particular path—which served as a most convenient short cut from one main road to the other—had merely come to be used by pedestrians, horses, bicycles, even the occasional motor-cycle. It was far enough away from Broadfields not to bother the Derwents, and Grayson, the edge of whose garden was a good deal nearer, had never seemed to object.

The result of this fairly constant usage, at least in weather like this, was to make the churned, muddy surface of the path slippery and dangerous. Nevertheless, Derwent made no attempt to avoid the hazards, though he did walk slowly, preoccupied. Soon he would turn north off the main path towards Broadfields house itself.

In fact, Derwent was wondering what in hell's name he could do. His appeal to Grayson had been a last resort, and it had failed. He must raise money from some-where—but where? There was nothing left to sell at Broadfields, nothing of such value that selling it would make any difference. The pictures were long gone—in his father's time—and the best of the furniture and silver.

As for Grayson's suggestion that he should economize—

that was a sick joke. He and Lorna had done nothing but economize ever since he'd responded to his father's appeal and left the army to come home and run Broadfields. But he couldn't have refused. Someone had to do it and Michael, who had never shared his love for the place, certainly wouldn't. Anyway, Michael was dead now, and the episode was all ancient history.

The estate hadn't exactly been a going concern when he had taken it over, Peter reflected sadly. And he was no farmer, and didn't profess to have a head for business. How could the place be expected to prosper under his management in these times? About the only part that was beginning to pay was the riding school that Clare had started. But it was only a drop in the ocean, and had no relevance to his present needs.

Peter Derwent's steps had been slowing, and suddenly he stopped completely. The whole wood shone white, and a deafening clap of thunder overhead coincided with the tearing crash of a falling tree. Derwent drew a quick, shocked breath. That had been close. Fifty yards or so further . . . What a fool he was to be walking through a wood in a storm like this. He should have waited at Grayson's until it was fully spent. Or, since that had been impossible in the circumstances, he should have taken the longer way home. If anything were to happen to him . . . He might not be worth much, he thought with a shaft of wry humour, but now all his life insurance policies had been surrendered he was worth considerably more to his family alive than dead.

Turning abruptly, he began to retrace his steps. He hadn't come far into the wood, and it was still worth while to go back, even though the rain was falling very heavily. If he had any doubts, another flash of lightning accompanied by an almost simultaneous roll of thunder quickly confirmed the good sense of what he was doing.

Derwent had no reason to suspect he had company in

the wood on such an afternoon, and the growl of thunder, the hiss of rain on leaves, the heavy creak of branches—all combined to conceal any tell-tale sounds. All Derwent knew was that at one moment he was hurrying, stumbling along the uneven, slippery path, intent on getting home. The next moment he was flat on his face in the mud.

For a split second he thought he had merely tripped. Then the pain sliced through him. He tried to get up on elbows and knees, but it was no use. He could taste blood in his mouth. A red mist seemed to swirl before his eyes. He made an attempt to call out, but no sound came from his lips. His breath was quick and shallow and he felt himself sliding into unconsciousness.

St Mary's church had once served a large and devout—or at least churchgoing—community, but modern times had changed all that. The congregation had shrunk drastically over the years, in spite of the efforts of the Rector, the Reverend Simon Kent. St Mary's retained a small, faithful nucleus, but had become mainly a site to be visited by tourists, admiring its eleventh-century stonework and its fine brasses and, it was hoped, making small donations to the perennial restoration appeal.

That Monday afternoon Simon Kent had been visiting an elderly parishioner who lived in one of the council houses on the left-hand road. Kent, who enjoyed walking, hadn't taken his car but, in spite of the heat and humidity, had strolled through the Derwent woodland. When the storm broke he was still with his aged parishioner, and he was faced with much the same problem as Peter Derwent.

The Rector solved it by staying to tea, and only when the storm had clearly begun to pass over did he set off for home. The thunder had receded into the distance and, though the trees were still dripping, he took the shortest way, through the woods.

Head bent, walking carefully to avoid the worst of the uneven surface, he was within yards of the prone body before he saw it. Horrified, he ran forward. At once he took in the small round bullet hole in the back of the bright oilskin and the spreading blood, red against the yellow. He knelt and pulled back the hood. Then gently he turned the head to reveal the long, handsome face, grey with approaching death.

'Peter! Dear God!'

Derwent had been sliding in and out of consciousness. Now he opened his eyes and through the mists he recognized his good friend, Simon. He tried to speak and Kent, seeing the effort, put his ear close to Derwent's mouth. He was just able to catch three words, Lorna, children—and a name, seemingly irrelevant. Then the eyes glazed and stared.

The Rector wasted no time in doing what he could. He found no pulse in Derwent's neck, no sign of breathing; he had no doubt that Derwent was dead, that any attempt at the kiss of life would be useless. Nevertheless, he slipped off his jacket to make a pillow for Derwent's head so that at least his face would be clear of mud and water. Then, pausing for only a moment to make the sign of the cross over the body, he ran as fast as he could for help.

CHAPTER 2

Instinctively Simon Kent made for his rectory. The old lady he had just left had no phone, and he couldn't go from door to door along the row of council houses searching for one. Grayson and his housekeeper might both be out, and valuable time could be wasted trying the cottage. After what he thought he'd heard Derwent say with his dying breath he didn't want to tackle the pub. And he couldn't go to the big house, Broadfields, breaking in on Lorna and the family before they'd had some warning of what had happened. No, the rectory was the answer; it wasn't much further than the alternatives.

Gasping for breath, an incipient stitch in his side, Kent was forced to slow to a jog. On the whole he was an abstemious man, though over the years he'd put on weight for he took no exercise other than gentle walking. Certainly he was in no condition for a hard run over slippery, muddy, uneven ground.

By the time he emerged from the dripping wood, he was sweating heavily, he could feel his heart thumping against his ribs and his breathing was laboured. He leant against the gate where the path entered the churchyard composing himself for a moment, then pushed it open. It squeaked loudly, and at once a small figure arose from among the tombstones.

'Hello, Mr Kent.'

'Holly!'

She was almost the last person Simon Kent would have chosen to come upon at that moment. Helen Derwent — usually called Holly — was thirteen, the youngest by six years of Peter Derwent's three children; perhaps the gap between herself and her brother and sister accounted for the fact that she was such a solitary child. In her brief pair of khaki shorts and a T-shirt with 'Derwent' stencilled across the chest, she could easily have been mistaken for a boy, except for her pony-tail of dark hair. And she certainly had no need to display her name so obviously. With that long, narrow face anyone in the neighbourhood would have known at once that she was a Derwent.

'Are you all right, Mr Kent?' She spoke with a curiously adult formality, regarding with concern his untidy grey

hair, his flushed face and the mud on his trousers.
'Where's your jacket? Your shirt's wet through and you've
been running. You look sort of — harassed.'

'I — I'm fine, Holly.' Impossible to explain. 'I — I had a
slight accident.'

It was a lie, but God would forgive him, Simon Kent
thought as with a wave of his hand he hastened along the
gravel path to the rectory. To his surprise as he fumbled
with his key the door was flung open and he was
confronted by his wife, Jean.

'You!' she said. 'I thought it was that Derwent girl
again. She was prettying up the family graves as
usual — morbid I call it — when the storm broke, and she
had the nerve to ring the bell and ask if she could shelter
here. I told her the church was open and she could go in
there.'

'Charitable of you,' Kent said, unsurprised at his wife's
reaction but nevertheless irritated. He had pushed past
her and was already at the phone. Since its expansion
Colombury had come to boast a fully-fledged police sub-
station headed by a sergeant, in place of the previous
single constable. Kent was thankful when Sergeant Court
answered personally. 'Sergeant,' he said quickly, 'there's
been an accident — a bad accident — in the Derwents'
wood, just beyond the pub. Peter Derwent's been
killed — shot.'

'Are you sure he's dead?' the sergeant asked at once.

'As certain as I can be. I didn't dare move him. But get
Dr Band and an ambulance and — '

'I know. I know, Mr Kent.' The sergeant's soothing
voice cut short the flow of words. 'Where exactly is the
body — Mr Derwent? And is he alone?'

Simon Kent explained briefly, and listened. 'Yes. Of
course I'll go back and wait till you come. There's one
thing. Mrs Derwent and the family — they know nothing
of what's happened and it would be dreadful if — '

'Quite, Mr Kent. Just get back there now and make sure no one else finds him and goes running to her. We'll be with you in no time.'

The line went dead and Kent put down the receiver. His wife was leaning against the door of the sitting-room, regarding him curiously. A tall, strikingly handsome woman, she wore her hair very short, and always dressed as if to emphasize the slight masculinity of her appearance. Now she shook her head.

'No, Simon,' she said firmly. 'If you think I'm about to dash off to console Widow Derwent, you can think again. You know we've never got on. I don't take kindly to being patronized by some so-called lady of the manor—'

'That's rubbish, Jean. Lorna doesn't—'

'Anyway I don't like her.'

Simon Kent bit back an angry retort. There was no time to quarrel, and he needed her help. 'All right,' he said. 'But go and tell Holly she's wanted at home—make up some excuse. She mustn't follow me back into the wood.'

'Oh, very well.'

Without waiting for more Kent hurried upstairs and collected a couple of blankets from the airing cupboard. He was shutting the front door behind him when he saw Jean returning to the house and, in the distance, Holly, pony-tail flying, running home.

'She's gone,' Jean Kent said. 'I told her there'd been an accident and her mother wanted her immediately.'

'You told her—' Kent began, and stopped.

Exasperated, he set out for the wood. At least Holly was out of the way. But there had been no need for Jean to frighten her, or to worry Lorna and the rest of the family. Time enough for that when they learned the truth.

The rain had ceased and the storm had passed, though the trees were still dripping and the earth wet and

muddy. Incongruously, the sun began to break through
the lightening clouds as Simon Kent reached Peter
Derwent's body. It was just as he had left it, apparently
undisturbed. Gently Kent removed his jacket from
beneath Derwent's head and put a folded blanket there
instead. He covered the body with the other blanket. The
gestures were quite pointless, he knew, but he felt that the
proprieties should be observed. Then he sat on a damp
tree stump to await the authorities.

He tried to pray, but prayer didn't come easily. His
mind was too preoccupied. Speaking to Sergeant Court
and to Jean he had called the tragedy an accident, but he
was almost certain that this could not be true. He knew
an entry wound when he saw one, and it was hard to
imagine how Derwent could have shot himself in the
middle of the back, accidentally or otherwise; besides,
there was no gun in evidence by the body. And the idea of
someone casually wandering through the woods with a
gun in the middle of a massive thunderstorm was equally
bizarre. Even if some such character had shot Derwent by
accident, why hadn't he tried to make his victim
comfortable, and then run for help?

But who would want to kill Peter Derwent? Kent
heaved a sigh. So far he had kept to himself the name that
Derwent had murmured as he died. If it had been meant
as an accusation, it was well-nigh unthinkable.
Wilson—Joe Wilson—was the landlord of the Grey Dove.
He ran the pub with great efficiency, and at the same
time cheerfully looked after an invalid wife. Admittedly
he had a reputation for being quick-tempered, and there
was no doubt he'd been annoyed when Derwent had
refused to sell him a parcel of land that lay between the
pub and Trevor Grayson's property. But that had been
months ago and, quick-tempered or not, Joe wasn't a
man to bear a grudge. As for deliberate murder . . .

Simon Kent's ruminations were interrupted by the

sound of voices, the shuffle of feet on the path, a muttered oath as someone slipped on wet leaves. Thankful to shelve temporarily the moral problem with which he felt himself faced, the parson got to his feet as Sergeant Court came in sight. Behind the sergeant were a constable and Dr Band, who acted when needed as local police surgeon.

'A great pity, Mr Kent,' Court said. 'I suppose he stumbled with the safety-catch off. That's how most of these accidents happen—'

The doctor, who had removed the blanket from Derwent's body and was crouching down beside it, interrupted sardonically, 'You're not suggesting Mr Derwent shot himself in the back, are you, Sergeant? It would take a contortionist to do that satisfactorily.'

'In the back?' Court bent down beside the doctor.

'This is how he was when you found him, is it, Simon?' Dr Band looked up at Kent, who nodded. 'You didn't move him at all?'

'I turned his head so he could breathe, and supported it.'

'He was alive then?'

'Yes—but barely, I think.' Kent waited for the next question—what, if anything, Peter Derwent had said—but to his relief it didn't come.

Sergeant Court's earlier somewhat casual manner had changed. He spoke quietly to the constable and produced a notebook, turning to Simon Kent.

'Exactly how long ago did you find him, sir?'

'Er—it must have been nine or ten minutes before I phoned you, Sergeant. That would make it about half an hour ago. I couldn't swear to it, of course, but I'm sure in my own mind I saw him die.'

The doctor had replaced the blanket and straightened himself. 'I suspect he'd been shot not too long before that,' he said. 'It was a small calibre bullet and there was a lot of bleeding.' He spoke matter-of-factly, but his round, reddish face was full of compassion. 'Poor old Peter,' he added. 'What a bloody waste. He was a nice man. And Lorna—' He turned away. 'There's nothing more I can do, Sergeant. It's up to your people now.'

The constable, who had been searching at the side of the path, interrupted. 'No sign of a gun, Sarge.' He looked hopefully at Kent. 'Unless the Reverend—'

'No,' said Kent. 'I saw no gun.'

The doctor and the sergeant exchanged glances. 'Right,' said Sergeant Court, 'I'll get back to the car and phone Kidlington. Constable, you stay here till they arrive. I imagine you'll be at the rectory, Mr Kent.'

'Yes,' said the Rector. 'Unless you'd like me to go up to Broadfields and break—'

'We'll go together, Mr Kent,' said the sergeant quickly. 'Perhaps you'd wait here till I've phoned from the car. And, Doctor—'

'I'm their GP,' said Dr Band. 'Lorna's a sensible woman, but perhaps I'd better come too.'

A moment later the sergeant was plodding back towards the road, while Simon Kent and Dr Band waited wordlessly.

'And what do you know about the Derwents, Abbot?'

Detective-Superintendent Thorne of the Thames Valley Police Serious Crimes Squad did up his seat-belt and leant back comfortably as the car driven by his detective-sergeant, Bill Abbot, left the Kidlington headquarters for Colombury. Other cars, with the scene of crime officer and a photographer and reinforcements, were already on the way, and the pathologist would follow as soon as possible.

George Thorne was a man of only medium height with a trim body, regular features, tidy fair hair and a neat military moustache. Neat, in fact, was a good description of his appearance—and also of his mind.

Abbot concentrating on the road, didn't reply at once. The question had been very general and he wasn't sure what kind of answer the Super wanted. Thorne, recently promoted, was new to Kidlington and Abbot, himself a cheerful extrovert, was still wary of him. The Superintendent was reputed to be a clever investigator, though sometimes not easy to work with; he was said to have an unfortunate habit of playing his cases close to his chest and keeping his conclusions to himself. This was the first case the two of them had tackled as a team.

'Come on,' Thorne said, a little impatiently. 'You must know something. They told me you were a local boy, born and bred in—what's the place called—Colombury?'

'Colombury. That's right, sir,' Abbot said with his soft Oxfordshire burr. 'And I've known the Derwents, or known of them, all my life.'

'Fire ahead then.'

'Well, when I was a boy old Gerald Derwent farmed Broadfields and his sister, a Mrs Nina Langden, kept house for him. The family's lived at Broadfields for ages and ages, but they've seen better days, and what with death duties and other things they're pretty hard up now. Anyway, Gerald Derwent died about six years ago, and his son Peter, who'd left the army by that time and was running the place, inherited.'

'Peter was the eldest son? The only son?' Thorne prompted as Abbot paused.

'No. There were two of them. Michael was the older, but he was already dead.'

Thorne stroked his moustache and waited. Abbot's intonation—perhaps his momentary hesitation—had alerted the Superintendent. There was more to come. Not, Thorne told himself, that it need be important. But he knew little about the case, and the more he learnt about the people involved—alive or dead—the better.

'Michael Derwent died a year or so before his father,' Bill Abbot continued. 'People said it was his death that finally broke up the old man. Michael was always his favourite, though God knows why. He was a villain, if ever there was one, always in trouble of one sort or another, some of it bordering on the criminal. He was picked up once or twice for the odd fraud or con trick, but never charged. When the UK got too hot for him he went abroad — Australia, Africa, all over. Eventually he fetched up with some mercenary mob in Africa. He got chopped in one of those tribal wars that was none of his business. I heard that Gerald spent a fortune getting the body brought home. He's buried in St Mary's churchyard with the rest of the Derwents.'

'Hm.' The Superintendent grunted. 'And now the younger son's been chopped too, as you put it. Not a very lucky family. Who's left?'

'At Broadfields? Nina Langden's still there. And Peter's wife, Lorna. And their three kids. Richard's the eldest — he's just finished at Oxford. Clare runs a riding school at the house — they've got stables on the spot. And Helen's still at school.'

'What about staff? Servants?'

'None that I know of, not now. Except for casual labour. Most of the land's been sold off or let, and all the Derwents muck in on what's left. They work damned hard.'

The Superintendent grunted again. Nothing that young Abbot had told him sounded particularly helpful or encouraging. 'Ah well,' he said at last, 'maybe someone was out after rabbits and shot Derwent by mistake.'

'In the middle of a bloody great thunderstorm?' Sergeant Abbot laughed with the Superintendent. 'We're just coming into Colombury, sir,' he added. 'We'll be at the station in a couple of minutes.'

CHAPTER 3

Holly Derwent raced home. Dashing into the kitchen, she shouted for her mother, but there was no answer and no one seemed to be around. She glanced into the large, untidy sitting-room where the family spent most of its time and called again.

Still nothing, and she ran out of the house towards the stables. Richard and Clare were in the yard inspecting one of the riding school's horses. Vain Glory, a roan mare with a dark mane and tail that Clare usually rode herself, had gone lame.

'You'll have to call the vet, Clare,' Richard was saying. 'Her leg's very hot.'

'Damn! I can't afford the vet again this month. He's been here twice already.'

'You don't have any choice.'

'What is it? What's happened?' Holly burst through the stone archway that formed the entrance to the stable yard. 'That bloody Kent woman said—'

'Don't swear,' Richard said automatically.

Clare produced a lump of sugar from the pocket of her jeans and gave it to the mare. 'It's Vain Glory. She's lamed herself somehow.'

'Glory? Oh—Is that all?' Holly sounded relieved.

Richard and Clare exchanged glances, half amused and half irritated, more concerned about the mare's lameness than about their young sister.

'You'd better phone right away. No point in waiting,' Richard said. He grinned. 'After all, you'll want Glory in good form when John comes over, won't you?'

'Yes, of course.'

Conscious of the flush rising in her cheeks, Clare tossed

the mare's rope to her brother and went along to the small office in a corner of the yard. She wished Richard wouldn't tease her about their American cousin, John Derwent. True, she'd thought herself half in love with John when he'd last visited them two years ago, but she was only seventeen then, and the letters they'd exchanged since had been merely friendly and affectionate — nothing more. Nevertheless, she had to admit she was looking forward to seeing him again.

Holly had followed Clare to the office. 'Do you know where Mum is, Clare?'

'Upstairs with Aunt Nina,' Clare said, beginning to dial. 'Aunt Nina's not too well. She's gone to bed. Mum's worried about her cough.'

'Oh dear! Thanks, Clare.'

Clare nodded and gave her full attention to the vet's secretary, now on the other end of the line. Holly wandered back to the house. This time she found her mother in the kitchen.

'How's Aunt Nina?' she asked.

'Not too good.' Lorna did her best to produce a smile. 'I'm afraid she's getting this summer 'flu that's going around. She's cold and shivery and that cough of hers is worse than ever. I've put her to bed with some hot milk and an aspirin.'

'Can I go up and see her?'

'Yes. You can take her this hot-water bottle. But don't stay if she wants to sleep.' Lorna filled the old-fashioned stone bottle, made sure it wasn't leaking and pulled a knitted cover over it. 'Here. Put it down by her feet. They were like ice.'

'Okay.'

'Thanks, darling. That'll save me going up again.'

When Holly had gone Lorna made herself a mug of instant coffee from the water left in the kettle, and sat down at the kitchen table. The coffee was hot and strong and she sipped it slowly, trying to relax.

Her back ached and she had an incipient headache. She hated thunderstorms. Today's had been particularly bad, and the heavy rain would have done the fruit no good. She ought to go down to the orchard and look at the damage, but there was the laundry to cope with and supper to be prepared. With Nina in bed she'd have to get the evening meal herself.

I wish Nina hadn't chosen today to be ill, she thought irritably. It had been a bad day, quite apart from the storm. A raft of brown envelopes in the mail—bills that had made Peter grimmer than ever; she had never seen him look more hopeless and dejected. Glory gone lame for no obvious reason. Holly at a loose end and obviously missing her schoolfriends, all holidaying in glamorous places. How lovely, she mused, to be by the sea, by oneself for once, away from the family and Broadfields and the constant crises and problems.

For a moment she gave way to self-pity, but almost immediately reproached herself. Work was the antidote. Rinsing her coffee mug at the sink, she went into the utility room and started sorting out sheets. She told herself she mustn't forget that John Derwent was coming to stay; she must get his room ready and think about food. Peter said they weren't to do anything extra for John, but of course they must. As soon as they knew exactly when he'd be arriving . . .

The doorbell rang as she finished with the sheets.

The moment she saw the three men Lorna Derwent was aware that something dreadful had happened. She knew them all, the parson and the doctor as friends, the police sergeant casually. Any one of them alone wouldn't have surprised her, but the three together, each of their faces fixed in a smoothly professional smile, made her quail.

She didn't show it. Outwardly calm, she said,

'Hello. Come along in.'

'Hello, Lorna. Thanks. Where are the rest of the family? All at home?' Dr Band took the initiative, following her into the rarely-used drawing-room.

'Richard and Clare are in the stables. Holly's upstairs with Nina. Nina's not too well. And Peter's gone down to the bottom field. Joe Wilson from the pub phoned to say a tree of ours was down across his property and Peter said he'd go and have a look.'

Lorna spoke quickly. She'd already in her own mind accounted for the members of her family, reassuring herself they were all safe. But as she turned to face the three men, her disquiet grew.

'Something's wrong?'

'There's been an accident in the wood, Mrs Derwent,' Sergeant Court began.

'An accident? What sort of—'

'Peter's been hurt, Lorna, badly.' Simon Kent went to her and put his hand on her arm to direct her to a chair.

She brushed him aside and spoke directly to the doctor. 'How badly, Dick? Where is he? I must go to him.'

'Lorna, Peter's dead.'

'Peter's dead? No.'

'He was shot in the back. In the wood. We don't know yet how it happened.'

'Peter's dead. Shot in the back.'

She was conscious of repeating words, but they had no real meaning. It was as though they were part of a language she didn't fully comprehend. For what seemed a long minute she stood and stared straight in front of her, a tall, thin woman in shirt and slacks, with high cheekbones, untidy dark hair and unseeing grey eyes. Then she drew a deep breath.

'Where is he now? Where have you taken him?'

'He's still where he was found, Mrs Derwent,' said the sergeant. 'There's a constable with him. In the circumstances, you understand, there'll have to be an enquiry.'

'Yes. Right.' Lorna clenched her teeth to recover her poise. 'I want to see him but—'

'There's no need, Mrs Derwent, not immediately. Identification—'

'Of course I must see him. Now. But first I must tell the children. Excuse me. I won't be long.'

Lorna's over-wide mouth twisted into a smile as she hurried from the room. They were kind, she thought, and anxious to be helpful. Later she might need their help, but right now there were some things only she could do.

She found the children in the stables. Not children any more, she reminded herself, as Richard and Clare came out of the tack room—except of course for Holly. Holly was desultorily sweeping the yard.

'Aunt Nina went to sleep, so I left her,' Holly said, abandoning her task.

'Good. She needs sleep. We won't disturb her.'

'I phoned the vet,' Clare said. 'The new man's coming to have a look at Glory's leg.'

'Good,' Lorna said again.

'What is it, Mum?' Richard, by far the most perceptive of the three, was frowning at his mother. 'You're very pale. Are you all right?'

'Yes. I'm all right, but—'

She told them simply, bluntly. Richard put his arms round her and held her tight for a moment. Holly clung to Clare, hiding her face. None of them wept.

Lorna said, 'I'm going with Dr Band and Sergeant Court to see—'

'I'll come with you,' Richard said at once.

'And me,' said Clare, raising her face from Holly's hair.

'No, no, darlings. Not yet. You stay here. You've got the vet coming. And there are the chores. Things go on. I—I've done nothing about supper yet.' She was speaking almost at random.

Richard hesitated, meeting Clare's eyes and understanding the immediate need for seeming normalcy. He
put out a hand and touched his mother's arm. 'Okay,' he
said. 'If you're sure. We'll look after everything. But what
about Aunt Nina?'

'Don't tell her. I'll tell her when I get back. It'll be a
dreadful blow to her.' A blow to us all, Lorna thought,
but in some ways worst for Nina, because she was old and
Peter had been like her own child. 'You know how she
adores your father.'

Richard nodded. 'And Uncle Tim? I should phone
him?'

'Oh yes, of course. Do that.'

Lorna remembered Tim Railton with relief. Dear Tim,
always there, always ready to help. He was no relation,
though the children called him uncle. He was in fact the
senior partner of a flourishing country law practice
centred on Colombury, and one of the Derwents' oldest
friends. It was through Tim that she'd first met Peter.
Which had been hard on Tim, Lorna thought, her mind
drifting into irrelevancies, because Tim had undoubtedly
wanted to marry her himself. He'd never married anyone
else . . .

'Mum!' Richard said sharply.

'Sorry, darling.' Lorna passed a hand over her face,
wiping away memories. She forced herself to smile at her
son, so like his father when he was that age . . . Later, she
told herself, later she'd mourn. Now she must be
practical. 'Yes,' she said again. 'Phone Tim right away. I
won't be long.'

As soon as their mother had gone Richard and Clare went
across to the stable office. Richard dialled Railton's firm's
number, and asked for him.

Tim Railton's secretary said, 'I'm sorry, Mr Derwent.

Mr Railton's not in today. He phoned this morning to say
he was unwell, probably this bug everyone's catching. He
thought he'd better stay at home. Unless it's very urgent I
suggest—'

'It is urgent, very. Thanks.' Richard put down the
receiver, cursing under his breath. If Tim was ill it was
unfair to ask him to come but his moral support, as well
as his professional help, would be invaluable. Richard
dialled Railton's home number.

The phone rang and rang, but there was no answer.
Frowning, he dialled again, thinking he might have been
calling a wrong number. He let the phone ring for a full
two minutes, then banged down the receiver.

Clare, who had been staring out of the window, turned
to her brother. She had been crying now, and her eyes
were a little red, but she was quite composed. 'No luck?'
she said.

'No,' said Richard. 'I can't understand it. His secretary
says he's got the 'flu, but there's no reply from his home. I
know he lives alone, but you'd think he'd be well enough
to answer the phone. We'll have to try again later.' He
removed a bridle from a chair and sat down, his head in
his hands.

'Richard,' said Clare suddenly. 'Do you think I should
cancel tomorrow's classes? We can't go on as if nothing's
happened when—when Dad's dead like this, can we?
And—and how many days should I cancel?'

Richard hesitated. No riding lessons meant no money
coming in, but horses still had to be fed, the vet paid.
Richard was as practical as his mother. 'Don't cancel
anything. You don't have to take them out on the road.
Keep them in the ring—or make them jump or
something.'

'You really think that'll be okay?'

'Here's your answer,' Richard said with unusual
bitterness, getting to his feet as a small van drove into the

yard. 'Think of his bill.'

For the next ten or fifteen minutes they concentrated on the vet and the lame mare. Then, when the van had driven away, Richard glanced round the stables. 'Where's Holly got to?' he asked.

'Back in the house, I think,' said Clare. 'I saw her go that way while you were on the phone. I expect she's in her room, having a private weep.'

'She shouldn't be alone, should she, not now,' said Richard. With one accord they turned towards the house.

In the hall they found Lorna with Dr Band. Before they could speak the doctor held up a hand. 'It's a little early,' he said, 'but I'm going to cadge a drink and prescribe one for your mother, and for both of you too.'

Lorna led the way into the family sitting-room. 'Where's Holly?' she asked.

'In her room, we think,' Clare replied. 'Shall I fetch her?'

'No, it's all right,' Lorna said. 'I'll go up myself in a minute. Dr Band's going to have a look at Aunt Nina and — and I shall have to tell her.'

In the event, however, this proved quite unnecessary. Richard had scarcely started to pour drinks when the sitting-room door was flung open and Nina Langden burst into the room, pulling Holly after her by one arm.

Her face was white and she spoke without preamble. 'It's not true what this wicked girl says! It's not true that Peter's been shot, killed?' Her voice broke as she released Holly.

Normally, even when she was wearing her oldest clothes, there was a certain elegance — seemliness — about Mrs Langden. But now elegance was forgotten and it was just an elderly, distressed woman who stood in the doorway wrapped in a drab thick dressing-gown, dark eyes wide and wet with tears.

'It's not true, is it?' she repeated.

'Nina, my dear, I was just coming—'
'It is so true. I didn't lie. Dad's dead.'
'Nina, I'm afraid—'
'Aunt Nina, it's dreadful but—'

Nina Langden stood quite still, seemingly forcing herself to accept the fact. 'Oh God!' she said at last. 'My Peter!' Then, mercifully, her legs buckled under her and she slipped to the ground in a dead faint.

CHAPTER 4

The police machine had swung into action. The photographer and technicians had done their work, the pathologist had been and gone, the body had been removed to Oxford, the area taped, the routine search started, and preliminary enquiries begun in the neighbourhood. In the midst of supervising all these operations, Superintendent Thorne and Sergeant Abbot had found time for only one interview that Monday night—with Simon Kent, as the man who had found the body. Thus it was the next morning before the two Kidlington detectives arrived at Broadfields. The storm had completely passed, the humidity had gone from the air and the weather was clear and sunny as they rang the bell just after nine o'clock.

They got no response and, looking about them, found their way round to the stables. Richard, in a disreputable pair of jeans and a filthy T-shirt, was mucking out the last of the horses. He'd been up since six after a miserable night and had not yet had any breakfast. As a result he wasn't in the best of tempers.

'Yes? What is it?' he demanded abruptly.

The Superintendent regarded him with a measure of distaste. Before Bill Abbot could intervene he said, 'I wish to speak to your mistress, young man, but no one answers the front door.'

'My mistress?' Richard's lips twitched as he thought of his current girlfriend. 'She's not here, unfortunately. She's away with her family in the Mediterranean.'

'What?'

Hurriedly Abbot said, 'Mr Richard Derwent, isn't it? This is Detective-Superintendent Thorne and I'm Sergeant Abbot. We're from Thames Valley Police, Kidlington. It's your mother the Superintendent wants to see, sir.'

Richard's face was suddenly bleak. 'Yes, I understand. I expect she was upstairs and didn't hear the bell. If you'll go round to the front again I'll let her know you're here.' With a brief nod he strode off and disappeared into the house through a side door.

'Arrogant young bastard,' Thorne said as he and Abbot retraced their steps. 'I suppose he thought he was being funny.' When Abbot didn't reply he marched up to the front door and kept his finger on the bell till the door was opened.

A young girl, also in jeans and a T-shirt, but with a long dark pony-tail, stood before them. 'Come in,' she said with some formality. 'I'm Holly Derwent.' She led them into the drawing-room. 'My mother won't keep you long.'

She waved them to chairs and sat herself on the edge of a small sofa, staring at them. Her fixed, almost imperious gaze made Thorne a little uneasy, though he would have hated to admit it. He glanced around him. A fine room, he thought, even gracious, though in need of redecoration. He could see signs of the Derwents' alleged difficult financial circumstances in the occasional bare patches on the walls and the slight lack of furniture. He wondered with some interest who would inherit. The wife? The son, Richard? He'd know as soon as he saw the will.

Holly broke the silence. 'You're policemen, aren't you,' she said, 'come to make enquiries about my father's—death?'

'That's right.' The Superintendent gave her what he hoped was a kindly smile.

'I was tidying the graves when he was shot.'

The smile vanished. Having already suffered from Richard's sense of humour, George Thorne was in no mood to be mocked by another Derwent, especially a girl hardly into her teens. Ostentatiously turning his back, he looked out of the window at the sweep of drive. But Holly persisted with her polite conversation.

'In the churchyard. I often go there. I like it. A lot of my family are buried there, though the only ones I knew were my Grandpa and my Uncle Michael. I look after their graves.'

The Superintendent could think of no suitable response to this piece of information, and continued to ignore Holly, wishing Mrs Derwent would appear and put an end to this waste of time. It was left to Sergeant Abbot to make some comment.

'Surely you didn't stay in the churchyard during that bad storm, Holly?'

'No. I sheltered in the church porch. I went to the rectory first but no one was home—not then. Later when I saw Mrs Kent come running out of the wood I went back. It wasn't—'

'What did you say?' Superintendent Thorne swung round.

'I went back to the rectory—it wasn't very nice in the porch—but Mrs Kent wouldn't let me in. She seemed angry, upset.' Holly shrugged.

'You saw her come running from the wood?' Thorne said. 'You're sure about that?'

'Yes. Why not? I expect she'd gone for a walk and got caught in the storm.'

At that point the door opened and Lorna came into the room. She looked pale and tired, but quite composed. The Superintendent introduced himself and Bill Abbot, whom she remembered, and offered their condolences. 'We're sorry to intrude on you at a time like this, Mrs Derwent,' he continued, 'but in the circumstances there are some questions we have to ask.'

'I understand. Do sit down. And Holly, you run along, darling.'

'Okay, Mum.' Holly slid off the sofa. 'Goodbye,' she added to the two police officers.

Abbot grinned at her as she went to the door, but Thorne's glance was speculative. 'Your younger daughter, Mrs Derwent?' he said. 'An appealing little girl. Truthful too, is she?'

'Yes — as much as most children are at her age.' Lorna's eyes widened in surprise. 'Why on earth do you ask?'

Thorne stroked his moustache. 'She was just telling us she spends a lot of time in the churchyard looking after the family graves. It seemed a little unusual.'

'Yes, I'm afraid it is. But it's absolutely true. She was caught there in the storm yesterday. She must have been there when — when Peter was killed.'

'Very sad for her to lose her father when she's so young. Very sad for all the family.' Abruptly Thorne changed the subject. 'This question'll seem very obvious, Mrs Derwent. Did your husband have any enemies?'

Lorna had been expecting something on these lines since Richard had told her of the arrival of the police, and she shook her head at once. 'No. Peter always got on well with people.'

'No trouble with neighbours?'

'No. Oh, there was a spot of bother a few months ago with Joe Wilson. He runs the pub, the Grey Dove, and he was annoyed because my husband wouldn't sell him a bit of land. But nothing serious.'

'And Mr Derwent's relations with his family were good, too?'

Lorna stared at Thorne coldly. 'Very good,' she said briefly.

'And apart from young Holly you were all at home yesterday afternoon?'

Sergeant Abbot was sitting unobtrusively to one side, but now he looked up sharply from his notebook. The Superintendent's line of questioning seemed a little direct at this stage, a little tactless when an important objective must be to ensure the cooperation of the Derwent family. Lorna's reply showed that she had appreciated the implications.

'Yes,' she said carefully. 'Clare, my elder daughter, brought her riding class in shortly before the storm broke, and Richard who'd been studying in his room went to help her with the horses. I was around the house. I'm sure you'll find we can all vouch for each other, Superintendent.'

Thorne ignored Lorna's last comment. 'And Mrs—Mrs?' He looked enquiringly at the sergeant.

'Mrs Langden,' Abbot said.

Dr Band had given Nina Langden a strong sedative the night before, and she had slept heavily. This morning she was relatively calm, and prepared to accept the fact of Peter's death. She had no temperature and her condition was clearly improved. But Lorna had insisted that Nina should stay in bed until the doctor came, and she wasn't having her disturbed by the police—especially by this officious officer.

'Mrs Langden was ill in bed,' she said. 'She still is. She's got this bug that's going round, this summer 'flu. The news of my husband's death hasn't helped. She brought him up, and she was devoted to him.'

The Superintendent, remembering what Bill Abbot had told him, nodded his understanding. 'We certainly

won't trouble her today then. You realize these are just
preliminary enquiries, Mrs Derwent? Maybe they'll prove
to have been quite unnecessary. Someone may come
forward and say it was an accident, but he panicked and
ran. That would save a lot of bother.' He permitted
himself a small smile. 'Do you keep any guns in the house,
Mrs Derwent?'

Momentarily Lorna, whose thoughts had been on
Nina, was startled. 'Oh yes. Yes. Most of the farmers
around here do—ordinary sporting rifles, you know, or
shotguns, licensed and everything. We used to have two,
but there's only one now. Peter shoots—shot—the odd
rabbit, and he taught the children to shoot. Tin cans,
mostly. But they weren't really interested.'

'I'd like to see it before we go.'

'Yes, of course.'

'Where do you keep it?'

'We don't have a gun-room, Superintendent. It's in the
office by the stables, in a locked cupboard. And we're
very careful with it, especially since the other one was
stolen last year.'

'Stolen?' Thorne was immediately interested. 'When?
And what sort of gun was it?'

'Shortly before Christmas. They were both the
same—Remington .22s, I think. One of them just
disappeared. Actually there were a lot of thefts in the
neighbourhood about that time and the police did catch
a man, but by then he'd sold most of the stolen stuff in
London. Some of it was recovered later, but we were
unlucky. I'm sure Sergeant Abbot must remember the
affair. It caused quite a stir in Colombury at the time.'

'Yes I do, Mrs Derwent. Indeed I do,' Bill Abbot said.
'The villain got a suspended sentence, as I recall—
mitigating circumstances, according to the magistrate.
Though how he managed to come to that conclusion, I
can't—'

His words tailed away as there came the sound of the front doorbell and, almost immediately, the door opening and someone calling, 'Lorna! Lorna! Where are you?' It was a man's voice, and Lorna recognized it instantly as Tim Railton's.

'Excuse me.' She was on her feet at once, relief shining in her face. 'Here, Tim.'

Lorna didn't bother to shut the drawing-room door as she hurried into the hall, and from where he sat Superintendent Thorne saw her run to Railton, who put his arms around her and held her close.

'Lorna, my dear! What can I say? I'm so sorry, so very sorry. Poor Peter!'

Their voices became lower, but the Superintendent moved quickly. He was seized by a sudden urge to study at close quarters a rather indifferent portrait of some former Derwent that hung near the door. He gestured to Sergeant Abbot to stay quiet, and from his new position could quite easily hear what was being said.

'. . . came as soon as I could, as soon as I knew. They told me when I got into the office this morning.'

'We tried to get hold of you yesterday, Tim. Richard phoned and phoned. Your secretary said you had this bug and—'

'Yes. I spent the weekend in bed and I felt so ghastly yesterday I decided to give the office a miss.'

'But you weren't home yesterday. Richard tried.'

'I was, you know.'

'Well, you didn't answer the phone.'

'My dearest, I'm sorry. I didn't hear it. I was in bed, doped to the eyes with anti-histamines.'

'Anyway, it doesn't matter. You're here now, Tim, and so are the police, asking all sorts of questions.'

Again Superintendent Thorne moved swiftly. He was back in his seat when Lorna brought Railton into the room and introduced him. A pleasant chap, Thorne thought appraisingly as they shook hands. Brown hair, brown eyes, spectacles, nondescript features. By no means as good-looking as Peter Derwent must have been in life. Surely not a lover? But Mrs Derwent's face had definitely lit up when she heard his voice, and there was something about the way he'd greeted her, held her, spoken to her . . .

Lorna had introduced Railton as an old friend and the family solicitor. Thorne said, 'I hadn't got around to asking Mrs Derwent for your name, Mr Railton, but of course we would have been coming to see you very soon. You have Mr Derwent's will?'

'Yes. I'm the executor.'

'Fine. Perhaps—if Mrs Derwent doesn't object—you'd be good enough to give us an idea of its contents.'

Tim Railton glanced briefly at Lorna, and then said. 'There can't be any objection. It's the simplest of wills. Apart from a few personal gifts—like his grandfather's watch which goes to his son—everything's left to Mrs Derwent.'

'And can you put some sort of value on the estate?'

Railton hesitated for a moment. 'I'm sorry, but I couldn't do that off the cuff, Superintendent,' he said. 'I shall have to look through the files, and—' Again he glanced at Lorna.

'That's perfectly all right, sir,' Thorne said at once. 'It was just a standard question. I'll come and see you in your office if we have to go into the matter in more detail.'

Railton said, 'Forgive me, Lorna.' Then to the Superintendent, 'I know Peter was shot in the back. Are you thinking of it as accident or murder?'

It was Thorne's turn to hesitate. Finally he said. 'We don't quite know yet, Mr Railton. But if it was an accident someone else must have been involved. No one's come forward and, if no one does, we'll be treating it as a murder case.' The Superintendent looked at his watch, and turned to Lorna. 'Mrs Derwent, before we go you said we could see your rifle.'

'Oh yes. Certainly.'

The four of them went in silence to the stable yard, where two small girls in jodhpurs and hard hats were being collected by their mother amidst a certain amount of confusion. The children said goodbye to Clare and waved to Lorna and were driven away. Clare was introduced to Superintendent Thorne, who kept a careful distance from the ponies she was holding, and to Sergeant Abbot. Richard came out of the office and, ignoring the policemen, greeted Tim Railton and exchanged a few sentences with him in a low voice.

Five minutes later, the rifle having been given a cursory inspection, Thorne and Abbot went back to their police car and set off down the drive.

'That was a quick departure, wasn't it, sir?' Bill Abbot ventured.

'Why not? We're busy men, lots to do. No point in wasting time.'

'No, sir, but—'

'But what, Abbot? Look, we've done all we can at Broadfields for the moment. We've met the household, except for the sick woman—and there was no point in making ourselves unpopular by pursuing that. We weren't going to get any more out of them, not now, not once that Railton chap had arrived on the scene to protect the family interest.'

'We could have taken the rifle, sir. After all, it was a .22 that killed Derwent.'

Thorne gave a thin smile. 'Sure, I know that. But I also saw it had been cleaned recently and was gleaming bright. I don't imagine it'll disappear when we want to have another look at it. And we've left them guessing a bit. It's a great mistake to show too much of your hand too early in an enquiry.'

Bill Abbot nodded a little doubtfully. As they rounded the last curve in the drive he slowed the car almost to a standstill and turned to his superior. 'What next, sir? Which way?'

'I think we'll go and visit some of the neighbours,' Thorne said. Then he looked ahead and added, 'And one of them seems to be waiting for us. It's that clergyman who found the body, Simon Kent.'

CHAPTER 5

The Reverend Simon Kent had been wrestling with his conscience. If either Joe Wilson or Mrs Wilson had been members of his congregation or more than the merest of acquaintances, he would certainly have gone to them and told them of Peter Derwent's last words. As it was, they had rarely been inside his church and, since Jean objected to his visiting the pub, he knew the Wilsons only slightly, and he couldn't bring himself to face them with what amounted to an accusation.

Nevertheless, Peter Derwent had been a close friend, and someone had killed him. Because of this and because in the end he couldn't be a party to withholding possibly vital evidence from the authorities, he had reached a decision. He must tell Superintendent Thorne what he'd heard Peter say, admit that he shouldn't have concealed it when he'd made his statement the previous evening and offer his apologies. He could only hope that Thorne would understand.

It was clearly the right decision, but he was reluctant to put it into effect. To postpone what he feared would be an embarrassing interview with the Superintendent, Kent walked across to Broadfields — a path led almost directly from the rectory to the house — to extend what comfort he could to the Derwents. He arrived in time to see the police car standing outside, and uncourageously hid behind a bush as Thorne and Abbot came back from the stables to tackle the front door for the second time. He watched Holly let them in and waited, hoping they would not be long. Then he saw Tim Railton arrive.

Frustrated, he walked down the drive and stood by the main gates. After a while he began to pace up and down. The grass was still damp and he couldn't sit under the trees. He was thankful when he heard a car coming and realized it was the detectives.

It drew up beside him. 'Good morning, Mr Kent.' Superintendent Thorne sounded positively jovial. 'Can we give you a lift?'

'Er—thank you, no, Superintendent. I was on my way to see if I could be of any assistance to poor Mrs Derwent, but I'd very much like a word with you first.'

'But of course.' Thorne got out of the car and, when Abbot had pulled in on the verge beside the drive, opened the rear door for the Rector and slid in beside him. 'What can we do for you, Mr Kent? Have you remembered something that might be of help to us?'

Sergeant Abbot caught sight of Simon Kent's face in his rear-view mirror, and grinned to himself. Clearly the simple question had caught Kent by surprise. He wasn't to know how often people 'remembered' something the next day. From the Rector's point of view, it was as if the Superintendent had read his mind, and he couldn't hide his consternation, his feelings of guilt. Poor bugger, Abbot thought, remembering the uncompromising Mrs Kent.

'Yes—and again no,' said Simon Kent. I didn't exactly forget what I'm about to tell you. I have to admit I—refrained from telling you. I didn't want to cast any suspicion on someone who's probably completely innocent.'

'I appreciate that, Mr Kent. However . . .'

'Yes, I know, Superintendent. I'm not a fool. That's why I've come to you now.' Kent was pleasantly surprised by Thorne's reaction to his announcement, but still he hesitated; he didn't like what he was doing. 'I told you that when Peter Derwent was dying he mumbled something about his wife and children. What I didn't say was that he—he also mentioned a name. It was the last word he spoke—'

'So?'

'The name was Wilson.'

'Wilson?' Thorne showed only mild interest. 'And naturally you thought of one particular Wilson, Mr Kent, or you wouldn't have been chary about informing us. I imagine it was the publican you had in mind—Joe Wilson, isn't it? We already know he had some kind of argument with Mr Derwent over a bit of land.'

Simon Kent nodded, relieved. 'Of course, I could be wrong,' he said.

'About what Derwent said?'

'No, no. I'm pretty sure of that. But Wilson's not an unusual name, is it?'

Simon Kent was clearly clutching at straws, but Thorne was prepared to humour him. 'No, indeed,' he replied. Then he leant across the clergyman and opened the door for him. 'Thank you very much for your help, Mr Kent. We'll be in touch with you if necessary. We won't offer you a lift if you're going up to Broadfields.' Automatically Kent got out of the car, and Thorne pulled the door shut and raised his hand in a half salute.

'Where to now, sir?' Abbot asked, edging the car forward.

'Let's try the pub, and see this Mr Wilson.'

'You think there might be something in it?'

'Might be. On the other hand, might not. Remember what that Holly child said she saw. Maybe Kent was trying to lay a false trail to protect his wife or something. Who knows? Come on. Let's get going.' The Superintendent smiled happily. The pleasant weather and the country air seemed to be improving his temper.

The Grey Dove, standing at the road junction towards the north of Colombury and at the southern tip of the Derwents' property, was an attractive pub of mellow Cotswold stone. It did excellent business; it was popular with the locals and, especially in the summer, had a flourishing tourist trade. Its success was largely due to the character and efficiency of its landlord.

Joe Wilson was in his early forties, a normally friendly, cheerful man, in spite of the burden of an invalid wife. If his temper was occasionally quick, he was always ready to offer a hand—and a drink—in reconciliation, and he would have claimed to have no enemies. He worked hard, kept on the right side of the law and had all the appearance of a model citizen.

Nevertheless, when he opened the door to the two detectives, Wilson immediately became wary. He hardly acknowledged Bill Abbot's greeting, though Abbot was a good customer when he happened to be in Colombury. Instead, he concentrated his attention on Superintendent Thorne.

'Mr Joseph Wilson?'

'Yes, that's me. My friends call me Joe.'

Thorne rather pointedly ignored this piece of gratuitous information, and with some formality produced his warrant card. 'May we come in, Mr Wilson? There are some enquiries we must make in connection with the death of Mr Peter Derwent yesterday.'

Joe Wilson nodded, and led them to a table in his saloon bar. 'We should be right enough in here. I'd ask you through to our sitting-room, but my wife's coming downstairs soon and I don't want her—worried. She's not a well woman.'

The Superintendent took the most comfortable chair
that was available and pointed to where Wilson should
sit. Sergeant Abbot took his cue from his superior and
retired to a window seat, ostentatiously placing his
notebook on the table before him. Thorne took his time.
'Nice little place you've got here,' he said con-
versationally. 'A free house, too, I see from your sign, not
owned by one of the big breweries. Big mortgage?' he
added suddenly.

'Nothing I can't cope with,' Wilson said at once.
'Business keeps up pretty well, and this is a good location.
I could sell out to a brewery any time if I wanted to.'

'But you're doing all right on your own?'

'Yes,' said Wilson shortly.

'I thought so. They tell me you've been thinking of
buying some land from Mr Derwent. That was to extend
the pub?'

Wilson shot a reproachful glance at Bill Abbot. 'Ah,
you've heard that story, have you? Yes, it's true. We did
have a bit of a barney over that land. I wanted to buy it;
still do for that matter. Not to build on, but it would
make a right nice place for drinking on a summer's
evening. I've even thought of serving teas and suppers out
there.'

'But Mr Derwent wouldn't sell. Why?'

'I don't know. I never discovered. He just wouldn't,
though I offered him a damn good price. Obstinate as a
mule he was.' Remembering how Peter Derwent had
thwarted him, Wilson re-enacted his anger. His blue eyes
gleamed, his mouth set and his jaw jutted forward. 'Said
it would spoil his property to sell. That was a load of old
rubbish! The bit of land lies between me and Grayson,
and Grayson had no objection. I asked him. I pointed out
there'd still be a nice belt of trees dividing us, and he
agreed at once. But Derwent—' Wilson scratched his

gingery head. 'It's not as if he was using the land for anything. I don't see how he could. In fact, it would tidy up his boundary if he sold it. But nothing would shake him.'

There was no doubt about Joe Wilson's indignation. But his very frankness — the fact that he made no attempt to disguise his feelings — told in his favour, and he didn't sound in the least rancourous, but merely annoyed and puzzled. Yet he'd been far from happy when the police had appeared on his doorstep, Thorne was sure of that.

Thorne said, 'Now don't take offence, Mr Wilson. We're asking everyone this question. Do you keep a gun?'

'A gun? No. Nor ever have. Mind you, I'll eat jugged hare or pigeon pie with the best, but I couldn't bring myself to shoot them — any more than I could shoot Derwent, Superintendent.'

Joe Wilson pushed back his chair and stood up. His earlier nervousness had gradually disappeared while he was talking, but it now seemed to return. He smiled anxiously.

'Joe! Where are you, Joe?' It was a woman's voice, thin and weak, but not in the least querulous.

'Coming, dear.' Wilson looked at the Superintendent. 'That's my wife,' he said unnecessarily. Then, aggression replacing anxiety, he added, 'She knows nothing about any of this and I'm not having her worried. She's a sick woman. I'll have to ask you to leave now.'

'Of course, Mr Wilson. Of course.' Thorne was on his feet at once. 'We can always come and see you again, if we need.'

Wilson went to the outer door of the saloon bar and unlocked it. 'I've told you all I know, Superintendent.' His eagerness to be rid of them was transparent.

Thorne gestured to his sergeant to go ahead. On the doorstep he turned. The door was already closing, but as if inadvertently he blocked it with his shoulder. 'Just one more thing, Mr Wilson. Were you at home yesterday afternoon?'

For a moment all Wilson's nervousness returned, and Thorne saw his Adam's apple move up and down as he swallowed. Finally he said, 'No, not all the afternoon. As a matter of fact, I went to visit my sister-in-law—that's my brother Ted's widow. I—I often do. She lives at Grayson's house. Next door to us, you might say. She's Mr Grayson's housekeeper.' Wilson was talking too much and too rapidly.

'Thanks.' Superintendent Thorne made no comment but set off down the path with a cheerful wave as the door closed swiftly behind him. He got into the car beside Sergeant Abbot. 'What's his missus like? A dragon?'

'Not from what I hear, sir. She isn't a local girl and she was taken ill not long after they were married, so no one knows her really well. Myself, I've only seen her about twice. But they do say she's a good woman, and there's no doubt Joe's devoted to her.' Bill Abbot started the car and looked his question.

'Grayson—and the other Mrs Wilson, I suppose,' Thorne said.

The two detectives sat in their car outside Trevor Grayson's cottage. Their repeated rings at Grayson's bell had brought no response.

'Pity,' said Thorne. 'I was hoping they might offer us a cup of coffee or something. It's time for my elevenses.'

Abbot grinned. 'We could try the old lady at Number Four.' He pointed to the row of council houses further along on the opposite side of the road. 'She's the one who entertained Mr Kent during the storm yesterday.'

Thorne agreed, but again they had no luck. The old woman wasn't letting them into the house. She'd already told the police that she'd asked the dear Rector to stay to tea when the rain came, and he'd not left till it was over.

She wasn't going to repeat herself, not for anyone.
Thorne thanked her politely and they beat a hasty retreat
to the car.

'She's helped to put Kent in the clear, anyway,' said
Abbot. 'We know from the water and mud under the
body that the shooting happened after the rain started,
and Kent found Derwent almost as soon as it had
stopped. It's hard to imagine the Rector picking up the
odd rifle between here and the wood, or planting one
somewhere on the offchance he might meet Derwent
there.'

'Ye—es,' said the Superintendent thoughtfully. 'Abbot,
tell me, who lives in that end house? D'you know?'

'No idea, sir. Why?'

'Someone's sitting by that upstairs window watching us
with great interest. Must be a good view up and down the
road from there. Maybe the character was on duty
yesterday. Let's go and enquire.'

There was an appreciable pause before the front door
of the end house was opened. A woman in her late
twenties, a toddler clutching her leg, another hiding
behind her, regarded them unwelcomingly. The shrill
screams of a baby came from somewhere in the back
premises.

'You the police again?' the woman said abruptly.

'Yes.'

'We've already had them. I told them I was at my
sister's yesterday. She lives in the town. I took the kids to
tea. It's not much but it makes a change, like.'

'There was no one at home then?'

'Only Gran and she's half ga-ga. My husband was at
work.'

'Gran's the one upstairs, is she? Can we talk to her?'

'Okay, if you must.' The woman shrugged impatiently.
'But I warn you, you can't rely on anything she says.
Gran!' the woman shouted as the two detectives crowded

into the hall with her and the children. 'Visitors for you!
Police! The room on the left at the top of the stairs. We
gave her the best one,' she added inconsequentially to
Thorne. 'Go on up. I've got the baby to attend to.'

Gran—Mrs Daley—was in her late sixties. She was
enormously fat and almost immobile but, the
Superintendent decided quite quickly, far from ga-ga.
She was, however, a lonely old woman and, given a
receptive audience, was prepared to talk at length—at
great length. Nevertheless, among the mass of chaff she
produced there were several grains of wheat, and Thorne
was glad he'd noticed her.

'My eyesight's still good, thank God, and I like to watch
what's going on. Why shouldn't I? Not that there's much
on this road. Nothing but cars, cars, cars. Now where we
lived before . . .'

To Abbot's surprise the Superintendent was very
patient. He waited till Mrs Daley had temporarily run out
of breath, and then said gently. 'You know Mr Derwent
from the big house, Broadfields, was shot in the wood
yesterday?'

'Of course I know. My son told me. There was a
policeman here asking questions, but he didn't talk to
me. Thought I was too old, I suppose. More fool him. I
was probably the last person to see Mr Derwent alive—
apart from the man what killed him, that is.'

'You saw Mr Derwent?' For a moment Thorne
wondered if he had misunderstood her.

'I wouldn't swear it was him. Not in a court of law. But
you see that path—' She pointed out of the window beside
her. 'That's the path he was found on, isn't it? Lots of
people use it all the time: kids, people taking a short cut,
courting couples, bicycles, motor-bikes—noisy things,
they are—horses from Broadfields stables. Well,
yesterday afternoon I saw a man come out of Mr
Grayson's house, walk along the road and turn into the

woods on that path. It was all thunder and lightning and the rain was coming down and I thought how foolish it was to go in among the trees like that but—'

'What makes you think it was Mr Derwent you saw, Mrs Daley?'

'He was wearing a bright yellow raincoat—that's how I could see him so clearly through the rain—and I assumed he was Mr Grayson. But the policeman told my son that's what Mr Derwent was wearing when he was shot . . .'

Again there was a long dissertation, but finally Thorne was able to ask, 'Are you sure he came from Mr Grayson's house?'

Mrs Daley gave the Superintendent a pitying glance. 'Unless he came up out of the drain,' she said caustically.

Superintendent Thorne ignored the laugh that Abbot hastily turned into a cough, and thanked Mrs Daley profusely. Because of the position in which Peter Derwent had fallen it had been assumed by the police that he'd been heading away from Broadfields when he met his death, rather than towards the house. Now it looked as if they could have been wrong, which might or might not be important. Either way they needed to talk to Grayson—and soon.

They were at her door, saying goodbye and repeating their thanks, when Mrs Daley said, 'The chap on the motor-bike might be able to help you. He went past just after Mr Derwent.'

Thorne drew a short breath. 'What chap is this, Mrs Daley?' he asked quietly.

'How should I know? They all look alike to me in that ridiculous gear they wear. I said motor-bikes use the path. Well, so they do, quite often. But there's one regular. Every Monday and Thursday afternoon it is. Always the same times. Someone rides a motor-bike out of the wood and goes off up the road—'

'Away from Colombury, you mean?' said Thorne.

'That's it. And a couple of hours later he comes back and goes into the wood again. It's not a real motor-bike. One of those wretched little putt-putt things — they make more noise than — '

'And yesterday — ' Thorne tried to stop the flow.

'It was just as usual, wasn't it? He came back a little while after Mr Derwent went into the wood and followed him with his bike.'

Thorne pressed her on the time but Mrs Daley, though she had plenty more to say, was vague on this point. The most the Superintendent could gather was that perhaps five minutes had elapsed between Derwent leaving the road, and the moped rider going after him.

'Phew!' said Thorne as the detectives left the house. 'That's made me thirsty. But first we must get on to Kidlington and see what the boys have made of the tracks on the path. Though I doubt if we'll get anything,' he added gloomily. 'The whole place looked to me as if a herd of elephants had been churning it.' He looked at his watch and went on more cheerfully. 'Then we'll find a pub — not the Grey Dove — where we can get a drink and have a good meal.'

'We could try the Windrush Arms, sir,' said Abbot. 'It's in the town — more a hotel than a pub, really, but their food's quite well known around here.'

'Fine,' said the Superintendent. 'We'll leave our next house calls till after lunch.

CHAPTER 6

'Oh God!' Lorna Derwent said, shutting the front door behind Superintendent Thorne and Sergeant Abbot. 'Tim, what's going to happen to us all? It's bad enough that Peter's dead, without that damned policeman suggesting—implying—'

'He's got to make enquiries, Lorna. We've got to face it that Peter's death wasn't natural.'

'I know. I know.' Lorna breathed hard. 'But I feel overwhelmed. There's just so much to do, to decide about. How to shield the children—especially Holly—and Nina. They expect me to be strong. Then there's the inquest, arrangements for the funeral, and money—what do I do for day-to-day money? And silly things like the storm damage—tiles off the roof and the fruit trees in the orchard. It's all too much when what I really want is to go away into a corner and howl!'

Tim Railton nodded sympathetically. Over the years he'd learnt to keep his feelings for Lorna under control, though it hadn't always been easy. He'd watched her work too hard, make do, forgo holidays or minor pleasures, grow to look careworn. He'd watched in silence, trying not to blame Peter, forcing himself not to interfere. But now . . .

He said evenly, 'This is an occasion for being practical, Lorna. You know you've always had a reputation as a practical woman. Let's think things through.'

Railton had been afraid she might break down, but to his relief she smiled at his remark. He urged her into the sitting-room. Her grief for Peter she would have to work out for herself, but at least he could take some of the burden from her.

'First, money,' he said. 'Till the estate is settled the executor can arrange for funds to be made available. So there's no need to worry. Just send any bills to me, or I'll collect them. Otherwise spend what you have to. I'll fix it with the bank.' He grinned. 'I'm sure you won't be extravagant.'

Lorna smiled a little sadly. 'I think I've forgotten how, Tim.'

Fleetingly Railton wondered about the size of the

estate. What he'd told Superintendent Thorne was perfectly true: Peter Derwent had been oddly secretive about his affairs and, even though he was the family solicitor, he really had no idea of his client's net worth. There might well be debts, even large ones. Railton remembered the fat, brown envelope that Derwent had asked him to keep with his will. He'd made a joke about it not being opened until after his death, but even at the time the joke had sounded a trifle forced.

'Now, the damage you mentioned,' Railton went on firmly. 'In the circumstances it wouldn't be extravagant to employ some extra labour if it's necessary. I'll get Castle's to come and look at the roof and Fred Mason can cope with the orchard. He's getting on, but he's competent and reliable. That'll leave Clare and Richard to take care of the stables and the riding school, while you look after the house. Lorna, dear—' He put a hand over hers and squeezed it gently. 'Don't worry about the family. The young are extraordinarily resilient, and Nina's tough. Once she's got over this damned bug she'll be all right.'

Lorna responded at once. 'Oh, Tim, thank you. It's wonderful not to have to feel totally responsible for everything. But what about you? You're none too well yourself, and you must be awfully busy at your office.'

'I'm fine now, and the office can tick along without my complete attention for a while.' Railton brushed aside consideration of his own problems. 'Next, Lorna, the inquest. It'll almost certainly be a mere formality— evidence of identification, and an adjournment for the police to continue enquiries—that sort of thing. But I'm sure we can arrange the funeral for next Monday. Now, who should be told? And what sort of notice would you like in the papers?'

Encouraged by Tim Railton, Lorna, who wasn't normally wont to vacillate, made decisions rapidly. They

were interrupted first by Simon Kent, who seemed more
in need of comfort than able to offer it, and then by Dr
Band. Leaving Railton busy on the telephone, Lorna
took the doctor upstairs.

'Nina, dear, here's Dick come to have a look at you.'

Nina Langden was sitting up in bed, listening to the
radio. She looked desperately tired; her eyes were red and
rheumy and her fingers plucked nervously at the sheet,
but she was no longer the hysterical old woman of the
previous evening. She had put up her hair and made up
her face, and her mouth was set in a grim, determined
line.

'Good,' she said. 'Lorna forbade me to get up till you'd
been, Dick, but I tell you I'm not staying here all day. I
know there's a lot to be done — there always is — and I'm
not so sick I can't help.'

'We'll see,' Band said soothingly. 'We'll see.'

'My poor Peter,' Nina went on, half to herself. 'Dear
God, it's hard to credit. I never thought he'd die before
me, and die violently.'

That's true enough of Peter, Lorna thought as she went
downstairs, leaving Dr Band with Nina. No one would
have expected Peter to die a violent death, to be killed.
Michael had been different. If you chose to be a mercenary
soldier in Africa, you asked for what you got. Yet,
ironically, there had been a rationale to Michael's death
that Peter's lacked. For as far as she could see Peter's
dying had been without rhyme or reason, and somehow
that made it even harder to accept.

Tim Railton drove fast back to Colombury, his mind
preoccupied. He didn't notice the police car driven by
Sergeant Abbot that passed him going in the opposite
direction. But Superintendent Thorne saw Railton, and
thought it worthy of comment.

'There goes that lawyer,' he said. 'He must have stayed

to lunch with Mrs Derwent.'

Abbot merely grunted in reply as he drew up in front of Trevor Grayson's house. 'Someone's home now,' he remarked. 'I saw a shadow at the window.'

A plump woman in an apron, presumably Mrs Wilson, opened the door to the two detectives. Her nervous, apprehensive smile made it quite clear that she knew who they were, and was expecting them.

The Superintendent didn't beat about the bush. He said at once, 'Mrs Wilson, I assume your brother-in-law, Mr Wilson from the Grey Dove, told you we'd be calling on you.'

'On me? No. No, of course not. Why should he?'

'He gave you as his alibi for yesterday afternoon.'

Mrs Wilson's eyes widened. 'Alibi? Joe doesn't need no alibi. If you think he had anything to do with poor Mr Derwent's death, you're quite wrong. He was here with me, in the kitchen, when Mr Derwent was shot.'

'And what time was that exactly, Mrs Wilson?'

Mrs Wilson hadn't invited them into the house but, now thoroughly flustered, two spots of colour bright in her cheeks, she backed away from the door, allowing the two officers to follow her into the hall. 'I—it—it was during the storm, wasn't it?' she stammered. It must have been, because it had begun to pour with rain when Mr Derwent left here. We suggested he might stay and have some tea, but he wouldn't—I suppose because Mr Grayson and him had had words and—'

'Mrs Wilson!'

A man stood in one of the doorways leading from the hall, and Thorne regarded him with interest. He didn't need the housekeeper's hurried introduction to know this must be Grayson.

'Come along in, Superintendent—Sergeant,' he said authoritatively and confidently, waving them to chairs in a pleasant sitting-room. 'I was expecting you. About poor

Peter, naturally. A tragic business. Tragic. Mrs Wilson
and I must have been among the last people to see him
alive.'

Mrs Wilson had seized her opportunity and disappeared, presumably towards her own quarters at the
rear of the house. Thorne didn't object. There was no
reason to suppose that her prevarications and anxiety
were in any way connected with her employer, and he
preferred to interview them separately. He said blandly,
'Mr Derwent was a close friend of yours, sir?'

'Not close, no, Superintendent. I wouldn't claim that.
But the Derwents have been very kind to me, very
hospitable, since I came to live here. That was over four
years ago.'

'You didn't know them before?'

'Well, I had met them—once. Trevor Grayson's rather
hard, expressionless face broke into a reminiscent smile.
'It was like this. I'd come across Michael Derwent in
Africa, and he'd urged me to call on his brother if I ever
found myself in this part of the world. So I did, only to
discover that Michael had been killed in some native
rebellion or other out there. But the Derwents were
welcoming, even though Gerald Derwent—Peter's and
Michael's father—had died just a few months earlier and
his affairs still hadn't been settled. Anyway, I liked the
area, so when I decided to stay in the UK and heard this
house was on the market, I leapt at the chance.'

'Very understandable,' Superintendent Thorne said.
He stroked his moustache. Somehow, at this first
meeting, he didn't take to Grayson, but he knew from
experience that personal likes and dislikes were usually
quite irrelevant; upright and law-abiding citizens could
often seem a good deal less congenial than the worst of
villains. 'And you've been on good terms with the
Derwents ever since, sir? No neighbourly differences of
opinion?'

Grayson shook his head. 'Not really, no. Though it's true, as Mrs Wilson said, that Peter and I had a stupid argument yesterday afternoon. I've regretted that bitterly since, of course. He might be alive now if he hadn't insisted on dashing off into that storm.'

Thorne waited, but Grayson volunteered no more, and the Superintendent was forced to ask. Grayson sighed. 'What did we quarrel about?' he repeated. 'Just a bit of land. Nothing important. It lies between my property and Joe Wilson's pub. Peter wouldn't sell it to Wilson, who's eager to buy it. Instead, he wanted to sell it to me, with some sort of covenant so that it couldn't be resold separately from this house. It's useless to me, Superintendent, especially on those terms, as I told him. In any case I don't have the spare cash.'

'Do you know why Mr Derwent wanted you to buy it?'

'He needed the money. He admitted as much. But he was averse to the land becoming part of the pub.'

'I see,' Thorne said, though he was not sure that he did. 'Well, Mr Grayson, thank you for being so frank with us. Just a couple more questions. Do you have a gun?'

'Only a shotgun. Peter gave me permission to shoot over his land.' Grayson paused. 'But I wasn't doing any shooting yesterday, Superintendent.'

'I'm sure you weren't, sir.' Thorne stood up and so did the self-effacing Sergeant Abbot.

'You said a couple of questions,' Grayson reminded the Superintendent.

'Oh yes. I was forgetting.' Thorne lied casually. 'Do you own a motor-cycle, Mr Grayson?'

If Thorne had expected to catch Trevor Grayson off his guard, he was disappointed. Grayson's surprise had every appearance of being genuine. He looked his amazement, and laughed aloud. 'Good God, no!' he exclaimed. 'I've not had a motor-bike for thirty years. Why do you ask?'

But the Superintendent was turning towards the door,

and didn't answer. He merely thanked Grayson for his cooperation, commented that he had no need to speak to Mrs Wilson again immediately and shepherded his sergeant out of the house.

'We'll try the rectory now, Abbot,' he said as he got into the car. 'I'd like a word with Mrs Kent. Maybe she'll tell us what she was up to in the wood during yesterday's storm.'

But at the rectory there was no answer to their knocking, and they took the liberty of exploring. They found the Rector asleep in a hammock slung between two large trees on a lawn behind the house. Some garden tools near by suggested that he'd had good intentions.

Thorne woke him by coughing loudly. Slightly disconcerted by the intrusion, Kent explained that his wife had gone to London for a couple of days, but would be back on Thursday.

'She goes for a few days at the beginning of every month,' he said.

'The beginning?' Thorne queried.

'Yes—oh, I see what you mean. Yes, this'll make her second trip this month, but I'm afraid she gets rather bored down here. She misses the theatre and art galleries and shops and all the excitement of city life. My last living was only just outside London.'

'Couldn't she find all those things in Oxford? It would be a good deal closer.'

The Rector didn't appear to be disturbed by so apparently irrelevant a question, and answered readily enough. 'You're quite right, I suppose. But she has a great friend in London and she likes to stay there. She drives herself, so it's no bother.'

'She has her own car?'

'Yes. About five years ago an aunt died and left Jean some money. It gives her a small income, not enough to make her independent, but—' Simon Kent stopped abruptly, aware that he was talking too much, allowing his private doubts and misgivings about his marriage to show. It was no business of the police if the Bishop now considered him only fit for a sleepy country parish, where his wife was unhappy and of negligible help. 'Anyway, Superintendent,' he added, 'none of this is of any interest to you, I'm certain.'

Superintendent Thorne was not so certain, but he didn't pursue the matter. He apologized for disturbing the Rector, and said goodbye. Back in the car, he looked at his watch, and remarked, 'Headquarters now, I think, Abbot. We've no time to do any more here today. All the reports'll be in by now, and there's the inquest tomorrow morning. We must make sure everything's set for that. We'll get an adjournment, of course.'

'Yes, sir,' Sergeant Abbot said. He drove in silence for some minutes.

The Superintendent looked at him. 'Something bothering you? You're looking worried.'

Abbot frowned fiercely at the road ahead. 'Well, sir, if you don't mind my saying so, you do seem to leave an awful lot of loose ends. You didn't ask Mr Kent about guns or motor-bikes, for instance. You never even asked for the friend's address.'

'I know, Abbot, I know.' Thorne permitted himself an unusually wide smile. 'I've said it before and I'll say it again. You get nowhere by going too fast. All we're doing at the moment is stirring people up a bit. Once they've had a chance to stew for a while, our job could be a whole lot easier.'

CHAPTER 7

Tim Railton would have much preferred not to stay to lunch at the Derwents, but it had been impossible to refuse. He left as soon as he decently could, his mind intent on Peter Derwent's envelope. In some ways he wished he had opened it before he went to Broadfields, but his one thought had been to get to Lorna.

Now he parked his car in the small courtyard beside the offices of Railton, Mercer and Grey in Colombury High Street, and hurried upstairs. Mrs Kirby, his secretary, was waiting to pounce with letters to be signed and phone calls to be returned, but he brushed her aside and went through to his own office — a large book-lined room facing the front of the building — firmly shutting the door behind him.

The envelope was buried at the back of the top shelf of Railton's private safe, where it had lain almost forgotten for nearly five years. Impatiently he took it to his desk and slit it open. Inside were two further envelopes, one addressed to Lorna, one to himself, together with a sheaf of legal documents. He looked rapidly through the documents, and his eyes widened in disbelief. Then he ripped open the envelope marked 'Tim' and extracted the letter it contained. He read it once, fast, and again very carefully.

Dear Tim,

If you have occasion to read this and the papers enclosed with it, you will know what I have done. Believe me, I did it with anguish and because I had no choice. I tried every way I could think of to raise money, but there was no alternative if we were still to stay at Broadfields. I'd already denuded the house of what was left of any worth, and sold off all but the fields and orchard and woodlands that surround it and add to its value. As you know, Dad neglected the place, and I was never really cut out to be what is euphemistically known as a 'gentleman farmer'. I had — and almost certainly will have if and when you read this — a lot of debts and a massive overdraft. I suppose I might have got some sort of mortgage on the remaining property, but I would never have been able to keep up the repayments. So there was no option, bitterly as I regret it.

I can only hope now that I'll live to a fair old age. After all, why not? I'm very healthy. By then the children will all be settled, let's hope. And maybe by then, though God knows how, I'll have managed to save a little for Lorna, in case she outlives me.

If, by some evil chance, things don't work out like this, I can only commend Lorna and the family to you, my dear Tim, who have always been such a good friend. In which case, try to forgive me.

Peter.

Tim Railton unclenched his teeth and relaxed his fists; as he read, his nails had been digging into the palms of his hands. Damn Peter Derwent! Damn him! Why had he needed so much money? How in God's name could he have been so thoughtless — so stupid? Not cut out to be a gentleman farmer, indeed! He wasn't capable of running a market stall, if these documents were an example of his judgement. The only explanation was that he'd needed the money in a violent hurry. But why? And what had he spent it on? Not on his property, for sure. And as for Lorna and the family, their situation didn't bear thinking about. Unless . . .

Railton abandoned his personal feelings in favour of his

professional duties, and began to study the documents again, reading them with the greatest care. Finally he shook his head; he could find no flaws in the drafting. He flicked the switch on his intercom, and asked Mrs Kirby to put through a call to John Derwent in Boston, Massachusetts, USA.

It was some minutes before Mrs Kirby knocked gently on the door and came into the room. 'Mr Railton!' She drew back in surprise. 'Mr Railton, are you all right?'

Tim Railton's face was buried in his hands, and it was pale when he lifted it. Mrs Kirby had been his secretary for a long time and he trusted her implicitly, but there were some things he couldn't discuss even with her. He smiled wanly. 'Yes, I'll be all right, thanks. It's this damned bug. It takes the stuffing out of one.'

'You ought to be home in bed, Mr Railton.'

'I dare say, but — What about John Derwent? Did you get him?'

'No, I'm sorry. I got through to his number — Directory Enquiries found it — but he's not there. I spoke to his sister, who said he left for Europe three weeks ago. He was going to hire a car and travel around. She guessed he'd be in England by now, but she wasn't sure. I can easily call her back if you want to leave a message.'

'No,' said Railton at once. 'That wouldn't do. I knew he was coming over here — he's due to stay at Broadfields some time — but I hoped he hadn't left yet. I imagine he'll turn up eventually. Till then . . .'

Lorna would have to be told, he thought, and Richard and the rest of the family. As Mrs Kirby left the room to collect the letters that had to be signed, he sighed and picked up the envelope addressed to Lorna. For a moment he was tempted to open it, and see what Peter had said in his last message to his wife. And, though his lawyer's instinct for propriety was strong, he might not have resisted the temptation if Mrs Kirby hadn't returned. Hurriedly he bundled everything back into the large brown envelope and put it in his safe. Then he turned his mind to other matters. Peter Derwent's affairs would have to wait till the next day.

The next day was again bright and fine; the succession of thunderstorms that had marred the summer seemed to have ceased, at least temporarily. It was a day to spend in the garden, Lorna Derwent thought, not in a coroner's office in Oxford, attending an inquest on one's husband. Mercifully, as Tim Railton had predicted, the proceedings had been brief and formal. Once they were over, Tim had driven her and Richard back to Broadfields. She would have liked to stay there, to relax a little, to change from the unaccustomed black suit in which she felt hot and uncomfortable. But, when Richard had got out of the car, Tim had insisted that she accompany him to his office in Colombury.

'You don't mind if I take off my jacket?' she said, as Railton drew up a chair for her before his desk.

'Of course not.' Railton went to a side table where Mrs Kirby had arranged a decanter of sherry, two glasses and a plate of macaroons. He poured the sherry and put a glass with the plate of biscuits within easy reach of Lorna, then sat down opposite her. 'My dear,' he said, 'here's Peter's will. It's short and simple, but I'd like you to read it.'

Lorna took the paper and began to read while Railton watched her. No one could call her beautiful, he admitted. Her dark brown hair was carelessly cut. There were lines at the corners of her serious grey eyes and at the moment her over-wide mouth was down-turned. But the wonderful clear skin that he remembered from her girlhood was still unflawed, and the fine bone structure of her face would never change.

He loved her. He always had, he always would. There

had been other women over the years, and once or twice
he'd thought of marriage. But, in the end, it had never
seemed worth while, not unless he could have Lorna
Derwent.

Embarrassed by his thoughts as Lorna looked up and
caught him watching her so intently, he said, 'As you see,
it's perfectly straightforward. A few minor bequests and
the residue of the estate comes to you. The trouble is,
Lorna, there may not be very much.'

'No, I didn't expect there would be, so don't look so
worried, Tim. We're used to being hard up. While Peter
was in the army we did reasonably well, but since we
came to Broadfields it's been a constant struggle, as you
know.'

Railton took off his spectacles and began to polish the
lenses. He said, 'Brian Curtis, Peter's bank manager, is
away on holiday, but I spoke to his deputy. Peter seems to
have had a large overdraft. Do you know if he had a lot of
other debts, Lorna?'

'I'm sure he did, though he didn't always tell me about
them. I got a bill this morning for that electrical work we
had done last January.' Lorna opened her bag and took
out the bill. 'Here you are. It says "To account rendered".
I thought we'd paid it.'

Railton nodded. He was not surprised. He replaced his
spectacles, sipped his sherry. 'I'll need to come and look
through Peter's papers some time, Lorna, and the sooner
the better. Would this evening be all right?'

'Of course, Tim. Whenever you like. Stay to supper. I'll
ask Nina to add some extra vegetables to the casserole. At
least she's up and around again, thank God.'

'Good. She's got a pension, hasn't she, from her former
husband? Any other money?'

Lorna stared at him, a little surprised. 'A pension, yes.
But if there was any capital originally I'm sure it went on
Michael and Peter long ago, just as Broadfields ate up the

little I had.' Lorna paused. 'Tim, why do you ask? What's all this about. Why did you make me come here to your office? Is it — are you afraid there won't be enough money for us to keep Broadfields? Because —'

'Lorna!'

She stopped, shocked by the bleakness of Tim Railton's expression more than by his sudden interruption. For a moment neither of them spoke. Then Railton handed her an envelope. 'Peter left this with me for you, Lorna. You'd better read it.'

'What —'

'I don't know what's in it.' Railton anticipated the question. He went to the side table and refilled his glass; Lorna had scarcely touched her sherry. Behind him he heard her tear open the envelope and he waited, watching motes of dust dancing in a beam of sunlight from the window. But the silence lengthened, and at last he turned.

Lorna was frowning at the single sheet of paper in her hand. 'I don't understand,' she said. 'He hopes I'll never have to read this, but if I do I must remember he loves us, and try to forgive him and help the children to forgive him. Especially Richard, he says. But there's no reason for us to forgive him, is there? He doesn't say what for, or what he's done. Tim, do you know?'

This was a crucial moment, thought Railton. He hesitated, and then decided he had no option but to be brutally frank. 'Lorna, it seems he's left it to me to tell you. I'd hoped that letter would explain, but —' He suppressed his bitterness. 'Lorna, there's something you must face. My dear, about five years ago Peter sold Broadfields — the house, the stables, such land as remained.'

'Sold Broadfields? Who to? Then why are we still there? But Peter would never have done that!' Lorna was totally incredulous. 'He loved the place too much — more than any of us except Gerald, certainly more than I did. It wasn't just duty that made him give up the army and come back when it was getting too much for his father. Michael wouldn't do anything. I remember thinking when we heard of Michael's death and knew that Peter would inherit when Gerald died that it was only right and fair. It really was Peter's home, He hoped it would be his children's home. He'd never—Tim, there must be some mistake.'

'There's no mistake, Lorna.' Railton sat down again and looked across his desk at her. 'I've studied the documents. Peter sold the estate on condition that he and his family could live there, rent free, until his death and for one year after that date. Then it passes in its entirety to Peter's cousin, John Derwent.'

'John! But how on earth could John—'

'It was John's father, Daniel Derwent, who bought it, in his son's name as it were. It's not completely clear to me what happened, but it looks as if Peter was short of money and appealed to his rich American cousin, Daniel. Possibly Daniel could have loaned Peter the money, but wasn't prepared to do so without some collateral. So they made this arrangement. Daniel may have thought he was being generous and, from Peter's point of view, at least it kept the property in a branch of the Derwent family. As you know, he'd have wanted that; his alternative seems to have been an outright sale to a complete outsider—a non-Derwent, if you see what I mean.'

Tim Railton looked across at Lorna with some concern, but her initial shock was passing and she was able to consider the situation more rationally. 'I see,' she said slowly. 'It's all very odd. I never met Daniel, but you're right when you say he was rich—I think it was his father who made a fortune in the States, and Daniel helped it to grow. But I do know John. He's coming to stay with us sometime soon, and he was here a couple of years ago — but he never said a thing about any of this; he never even hinted that he might eventually own Broadfields.'

'Perhaps he didn't know then. Daniel may not have told him. But he must know by now. He must have found out when his father died — last year, wasn't it?'

'That's right,' Lorna said absently. She shook her head in bewilderment. 'Tim, I still can't believe it. Poor Richard! And Nina, after all this time. And the girls. What on earth shall we do?'

'My dear, there's no need to make decisions yet. When we've got a better idea how much money there's going to be —'

'Money!' Lorna interrupted. 'The money Peter got for Broadfields. It must have been a huge amount.'

'A hundred thousand pounds, as far as I can see. It was most likely a fair price at the time. The house wouldn't have been easy to sell on the open market.'

'And what's happened to it, the money? It must be somewhere, unless it was spent.'

'I don't know, Lorna. Maybe when I've been through Peter's papers —'

'Yes.' Lorna produced a crooked smile that wasn't reflected in her eyes. 'Tim, I'll have to tell them — Nina and the children. They've got to know. It's only fair.'

'Not immediately. Wait, Lorna, at least until this evening. Then if you like I'll tell them, as Peter's executor.' Railton returned her smile. 'They might find it a little easier to accept, coming formally from me.'

Nothing would really make it easier for them to accept, Lorna Derwent thought as she turned her old Mini into the drive leading to Broadfields. How could it? Nina, apart from a few brief years, had lived there all her life. And the children, even before Peter left the army, had spent all their holidays there. To them Broadfields was synonymous with home.

For herself things were a little different. As she rounded the last curve of the drive, she regarded the house without personal affection. Built in the middle of the nineteenth century, when servants were easy to get, it was now much too big, too inconvenient and it lacked most modern amenities. Yet even she couldn't imagine the family living anywhere else.

She parked the car and went through into the kitchen where Nina was preparing to make jam. 'Hello, where's everyone?'

'Richard's trying to study. Clare's teaching some child the first principles of dressage, and Holly's helping old Fred Mason to pick fruit.' Nina gave Lorna a shrewd glance. 'You look all in, dear. Let me get you some lunch—there's cold meat and salad—then go and have a rest.'

'No, I don't want any lunch, thanks. I had some sandwiches with Tim,' Lorna lied. 'He's coming to supper this evening, by the way. He's got to go through Peter's papers. I'll just go up and get out of this hot suit.'

But, alone in her room, her clothes discarded, she felt suddenly desolate. Flinging herself on the bed she had shared so long with Peter, Lorna wept.

CHAPTER 8

While Lorna Derwent lay on her bed, exhausted after her storm of weeping, Tim Railton was in his office facing his first formal interview with the police. He spoke frankly about Peter's last letters and the sale of Broadfields, but had some difficulty in explaining to the Superintendent's satisfaction why he had not mentioned the envelope at their earlier meeting.

'All right, Mr Railton,' Thorne said finally. 'Let's take

it that you didn't want to raise the matter in front of the widow until you'd had a chance to examine the situation. Now, let me make sure I've got things right. Peter Derwent inherited the estate from his father about six years ago, and sold it a year later?'

'That's it,' said Railton. 'Actually Gerald Derwent's main beneficiary was really Michael, and Peter only came into it if Michael died first. But, as you know, he did. In any case, once Peter had come home to take care of the estate, I suspect that Gerald meant him to have it, though he never got around to changing his will. In the end, of course, it didn't matter.'

'I see,' said Thorne. 'And the present size of the estate?'

'That I'm afraid I still can't estimate. It's going to take a day or two to sort things out.'

The Superintendent eyed him speculatively. 'Well, I'd be glad of an approximate figure as soon as possible,' he grunted. 'But I don't think we need trouble you any more right now. We'll be in touch. Thank you.'

It was a slightly ominous note on which to depart, thought Railton, as he watched from his window as the two officers walked along Colombury High Street towards the police station. In fact, Thorne was saying, 'We make progress, Abbot. That's given us a couple more names to think about.'

Abbot glanced at him doubtfully. 'A couple, sir?'

'Yes. We'll talk about it on the way to Kidlington. Think it over, Abbot, while I go and have a word with Sergeant Court. Tomorrow's Thursday, and we're going to need some help if our trap's going to work.' Thorne neatly side-stepped a pram that threatened to run him down. 'You get the car.'

'Yes, sir,' said Abbot obediently. As far as he could tell, the talk with Railton had provided one additional suspect. Who the hell was Thorne's second candidate? And what was all this about a trap?

Abbot sighed. George Thorne wasn't an easy man to work with, he thought. His prim, precise appearance suggested he would be dull, plodding, conventional. In fact, he was quite the reverse. You could never be sure what he'd do next. Maybe this got results, but it certainly made life difficult for his colleagues.

The sudden reappearance of the Superintendent at the window of the car carrying a large potted azalea served only to confirm Sergeant Abbot's impressions. The Sergeant opened the door and took the plant while Thorne inserted himself into his seat.

'It's my wife's birthday,' the Superintendent explained. 'That's why we're having an early night tonight.' Thorne did up his seat-belt, settled himself comfortably and held out his hand for the plant. 'Now,' he said suddenly, 'what about these suspects of ours?'

Abbot's grin faded. The Superintendent might look a trifle odd nursing an azalea in the front seat of a police car, but his mind was clearly still on the job. Abbot hesitated a moment, pretending a need to concentrate on the traffic. Then he said, 'I've just added John Derwent, of course. He seems set to gain a lot, and he's apparently swanning round Europe somewhere.'

'Yes, yes.' Thorne was impatient. 'Who else?'

'There's Mrs Kent, I suppose. It looks as if she was in the wood at the right time. And Joe Wilson. He certainly quarrelled with Derwent, and he seems scared stiff of us.'

'And?'

'There's this mysterious character with the moped. Pity we couldn't get anything out of the tracks in the wood, sir.'

'Yes. We'll have another go at the experts when we get to headquarters, but it won't help. It was the storm that made the difference. No one can tell for sure who or what was coming or going, or when.'

'But we knew all about Mrs Kent and Joe Wilson and

the motor-bike man before we went to the lawyer's. What's happened there to make you add—'

'Think, man, think!' The Superintendent now seemed in an excellent humour.

Bill Abbot hooted irritably at a car that had cut in rather too sharply ahead of them. He didn't much like guessing games of this kind. 'You don't mean Mr Railton himself, do you, sir?'

'No, I don't, though I'm keeping him in mind. I'd be prepared to bet he's in love with the widow, which gives him something of a motive. And we've only his word he was ill in bed at the relevant time. Odd he didn't hear that phone ringing.'

The Superintendent clutched at his azalea as the car went round a sharp curve. 'Careful, Sergeant,' he said. 'Mind my plant.' Abbot slowed slightly, and said, 'There's Grayson—'

'Exactly,' interrupted Thorne. 'Think what the lawyer told us about Derwent. Five years ago Derwent sold his house and land—including the bit between Grayson's property and the pub. That was why he couldn't sell it to Wilson when Wilson wanted it. But neither could he sell it to Trevor Grayson—'

'So Grayson lied to us,' Abbot said.

'It would seem likely, wouldn't it? Grayson admitted he and Derwent had an argument. He couldn't conceal that, because Mrs Wilson overheard them having words, as she put it. But it's hard to see how the argument could have been about that bit of land.'

Abbot took the bull by the horns. 'You think Grayson might have nipped out of the house without Mrs Wilson noticing—and shot Derwent.'

Thorne smiled. 'Not really, Abbot. Somehow I doubt if it's as simple as that. But if Grayson was prepared to lie to us, calmly and deliberately—quite differently from the way his poor housekeeper told her fibs—he's worth considering, don't you think?'

Abbot nodded, and for the next few miles Superintendent Thorne remained silent, apparently deep in
thought. Abbot didn't disturb him, though nothing had
been said about tomorrow's so-called trap. Instead the
Sergeant, being unmarried, was able to debate with
himself how best to spend his unexpected early evening.

They were approaching Kidlington when Thorne
roused himself and suddenly remarked, 'I said earlier that
our talk with Railton opened up a whole new vista. Has it
occurred to you, Abbot, that this Peter Derwent wasn't
quite the straightforward character his family and friends
and everyone thought him? On the contrary, he was a
devious chap who'd been deceiving them all—even his
wife—for a very long time. Possibly that's why he died.'

Abbot could think of no useful reply, and the
Superintendent again lapsed into a silence that lasted till
they reached their headquarters.

Not much later, Tim Railton arrived at Broadfields.
Unlike Superintendent Thorne and Sergeant Abbot, he
was not looking forward to his evening. Though he
wouldn't have described Peter Derwent as devious, he did
feel deceived, both as Peter's solicitor and as his friend.
And he was troubled by the possibility that there might be
more unexpected disclosures to come.

Lorna gave him the keys, and went with him across the
stable yard, where Clare and Richard were busy with the
horses, to the office. She had recovered from the fit of
weeping that had shaken her earlier, and was her usual
calm, competent self. 'We'll eat at seven-thirty, Tim, if
that's all right with you,' she said.

'Fine. With luck I'll be finished by then.' Railton
looked around the small, rather untidy room, at the
battered desk, the old-fashioned wooden filing cabinet,
the almost antique iron safe and the two built-in

cupboards. 'Everything's here, is it?' he asked. 'Peter didn't keep any special papers in the house?'

'No. Everything's here.'

'He didn't have a safe-deposit box, by any chance? There aren't any at his usual bank in Colombury, but he could have rented one somewhere else.'

Lorna looked surprised. 'Not to my knowledge, he didn't. And surely if he did the key would be among those.'

'You're quite right, Lorna,' Railton said. 'Certainly none of these look as if they'd fit a deposit box. Now, I asked you before about life insurance, and you said his policies had been surrendered some time ago. You're sure of that?'

Again Lorna was surprised. 'Quite sure, Tim. We discussed the matter. It was nearly six years ago, not long after his father died. We needed — Peter said we needed the money.'

Lorna hesitated, but Railton had turned to the desk and it was obvious he wanted to be left alone. 'I'll send you over a drink later,' she said.

'Thanks,' Railton said absent-mindedly.

As soon as Lorna had gone he decided to start on the safe. He unlocked it easily enough, but its contents proved uninteresting. Birth, marriage, death certificates, Derwent family papers. Railton riffled through them quickly before starting on the desk drawers. These, he discovered, were unlocked and untidy, containing a mixture of odds and ends, writing-paper, government forms, a few old betting slips — nothing of any conceivable interest.

Sighing, Railton turned to the filing cabinet. To his surprise, here everything appeared to be well-ordered. Papers relating to the stables and riding school, to Broadfields and its produce, to personal matters such as the children's school fees, receipts, bills, orders, accounts,

income tax returns, catalogues, correspondence—all
were in their appropriate places. A locked deed box in the
bottom drawer contained bank statements and cancelled
cheques dating back some years.

But it soon became apparent that this businesslike
façade was deceptive, at least financially. To put it
bluntly, Derwent had been living from hand to mouth,
robbing one account to settle another, taking money
where he could find it. If a gas bill had to be paid, he
would borrow from the riding school, and the vet could
wait. If the apple crop was early and profitable, he would
use the money for his most pressing creditors, and this
time the vet might be lucky.

It was a haphazard way of life that was completely
foreign to all Railton's instincts, as well as to his legal
training, and he wasn't surprised it hadn't worked. In
short, Peter Derwent had left a mass of debts, some large,
some ludicrously small, and, as far as Railton could see,
very little to meet them. With the main asset—
Broadfields—already disposed of, the Derwent family
would be lucky to pay off the rest of the debts, even after
selling up everything they possessed—horses, equipment,
furniture, everything.

Railton leaned back in his chair as Richard appeared
with a tankard of beer. Murmuring his thanks, he drank
half of it as Richard, after a curious glance at the papers
scattered over the desk, tactfully disappeared. Alone
again, Railton considered the situation. What was
missing so far was any indication of why Derwent had
been so desperately in need of such a large sum of money
five years ago, and what on earth he'd done with it.

Something was nagging at Railton. He'd been through
the bank statements once, of course, and now began to
examine them again in more detail. Yes! That was it! For
the past four and a half years there had been a regular
debit of two hundred pounds on the first of each month.

As usual, the statements were totally uninformative, but each such debit was marked 'SO' so presumably the payments had been made in response to a Standing Order.

Railton stared at the statements in puzzlement. It wasn't a huge sum — it certainly wouldn't have kept the Derwents out of the red — and there could be a simple explanation for it. But, if so, why hadn't he come across some reference to it among the other papers? He would have to ask Lorna.

But Lorna, coming to fetch Railton, could offer no explanation. 'Maybe the bank would know,' she said.

'Yes. But I think I'll wait till the beginning of the week, when Brian Curtis is back. His deputy's comparatively new, and he isn't terribly forthcoming.' Railton looked at his watch. 'Supper already?'

'Not exactly. I came to warn you. Simon Kent's here, with Dick Band. And Trevor Grayson. Will you come and have a drink with them?'

'Good Lord!' said Railton. 'What are they — a deputation?'

Lorna laughed. 'No. It's just that people are kind, Tim, overwhelmingly so. We're all invited to the Bands for Sunday dinner. Simon's taking a lot of trouble over Peter's funeral service. And Trevor says if there's anything he can do we've only to let him know. Even Joe Wilson phoned to tell me he'd deal with the tree that came down on his land, and I wasn't to worry.'

'Nice of him.' Railton smiled absently. His mind was still preoccupied with that curious regular monthly debit. It was the only constant in Peter Derwent's otherwise casual financial arrangements. Even Lorna's house-keeping money and the children's allowances had fluctuated as the family's fortunes changed, almost from day to day.

'. . . haven't found anything yet about the money Peter

got for Broadfields, have you, Tim?' Lorna interrupted his thoughts.

Railton shook his head. 'No, not a clue, my dear. I think I can account for a few thousands of it, but the bulk seems to have disappeared into thin air. However, I haven't finished yet. There are various avenues to explore. The London solicitor who acted for Peter over the sale may be able to help. So may John Derwent when he turns up.'

Railton stopped speaking as they entered the drawing-room. He was glad to avoid more questions from Lorna, because he didn't want to commit himself. He wanted to mull over what he'd learnt, and consider if there was some way, without infringing his professional ethics or arousing Lorna's suspicions, he could bolster with his own money what little capital Peter Derwent might have left.

He greeted the three men who were talking to Nina. Seemingly, they were awaiting Lorna's return, because as soon as she appeared both Grayson and the doctor got to their feet.

'I've got to be going,' Trevor Grayson said. 'I'm off to London first thing in the morning. Business appointments, mixed, I hope, with a little pleasure.' He turned to Lorna. 'I'll make a point of returning over the weekend, naturally, so as to be here on Monday.'

'Thank you.' Lorna smiled warmly. She didn't care a damn whether Trevor Grayson was at Peter's funeral or not. She didn't particularly like him. But she was sorry for him. She had always had the impression that, because of his acquaintance with Michael, he looked upon himself as a family friend, but that the Derwents had never really accepted him as they did, say, Dick Band or Simon Kent. 'Thank you, Trevor,' she repeated. 'We'd appreciate that.'

'And, remember, if there's anything—' he said.

'I must be off, too,' Dick Band said. 'If you walked over

I'll give you a lift, Trevor. You too, Simon.'

Simon Kent was more reluctant to leave, to return to his empty rectory, but Lorna, seeing that Nina was about to ask him to stay and eat with them, intervened hurriedly. 'I'll see you all out, then, and thank you for coming.'

'Business after supper,' Railton explained to Nina, who had looked her surprise at Lorna's unusual lack of hospitality. He smiled, he hoped reassuringly. 'Peter's will and suchlike.'

Nina looked up sharply. 'I suppose there's no money,' she said.

'I can't be definite yet — but, no, not too much.'

'It wasn't to be expected,' Nina said, as Lorna came back and Railton stood up, relieved.

But Lorna said, 'Tim, I think Nina should know about Broadfields before we tell the children.'

'All right.'

It had been bad enough telling Lorna, Railton thought, but somehow Nina was worse. Perhaps because she was a Derwent, perhaps because she was far from young and Broadfields inevitably meant so much to her, he felt that what he had to say, coming on top of Peter's death, would be almost insupportable. Steeling himself, he spoke bluntly.

Nina's reactions were unsurprising — shock, disbelief, anger. 'I can't believe it, Tim. Not Broadfields. Oh, it's no great manor house or stately home and a hundred and fifty years is nothing, but a Derwent built the place and it's always been ours.'

'A Derwent will still own it, Nina,' Railton said gently.

'But it won't be Richard.' Nina was suddenly fierce. 'It should be Richard's. Why didn't Peter tell me anything about this? He never so much as hinted. He mentioned the — the shortage of money. But not this — not selling our home.'

'He never told me, either,' Lorna said, her voice without irony.

Nina paid her no attention. 'Poor Richard!' she said. 'Poor Richard! What will he do?'

Later that evening Richard Derwent answered Nina's question for himself. 'Become a damned good lawyer, I hope,' he said, 'and without the encumbrance of this place around my neck. Truly, I don't mind for myself. I realize it's tough on you, Mum, and Aunt Nina. Maybe—maybe we can rent the house from John for a while—if he's willing.'

'That's an idea! If I can go on running the stables—' Clare didn't complete the sentence. Still trying to absorb the fact that Broadfields belonged to John Derwent, she was eager to be practical, but she had seen the involuntary shake of Tim Railton's head.

'It's no use making plans at the moment,' Railton said. 'Not until John Derwent's been consulted and we know the true worth of the estate.'

But if they couldn't make plans they could at least talk of possibilities. In fact, nothing would stop them. It was a way of encouraging each other. And, after a little while, Lorna and Railton joined in. Only Nina went off to her room to nurse her grief in private, and Holly sat silent. She was biting the end of her thumb, a childish habit she'd discarded years ago.

CHAPTER 9

Holly Derwent sat on the low stone wall that surrounded the churchyard. She was biting her thumb again, and drumming with her heels. Otherwise she stared solemnly at the men digging her father's grave.

From time to time the elder man, resting his back, glowered at her. He had already told her to be off, to get out of their way, to stop asking so many questions, and she had retreated — but only as far as the wall. And there she sat, watching them.

The men found it irritating. The day was hot — another thunderstorm was probably beginning to brew — but the ground hadn't fully dried after the recent rain, and was heavy to dig. Somehow the watching child made it impossible for them to rest on their spades for more than the briefest of intervals, and they were being paid by the hour.

They were not alone in finding Holly an irritation. From an upstairs window of the rectory Jean Kent had seen her, first talking to the men, then sitting on the wall. Mrs Kent, who had returned from London that morning after a fairly unsuccessful trip, was not in the best of tempers.

'Simon!' she called angrily, 'Simon, that Derwent child's making a nuisance of herself, annoying the grave-diggers. Do go and chase her out of the churchyard.'

The Rector protested. 'She's not doing any real harm, Jean.' He attempted a joke. 'Maybe they'll keep at it while she's got an eye on them.'

His wife was not to be placated. 'It's not right for her to be there. It's morbid,' she said. And when her husband made no move, she added, 'Very well, if you won't, I'll go myself.'

Her anger now multiplied, Jean Kent stormed out of the house and strode purposefully down the gravel path. Holly saw her coming and slid off the wall. She was smiling.

'Holly, you shouldn't be here, especially now. Run along home at once.'

'Why? Has there been another accident?' Holly continued to smile, in apparent innocence. She said, 'I was here on Monday when my dad was killed and I saw you come running out of the wood. I told the police about it.'

Jean Kent's anger exploded. 'You—what? You told the police? You little bitch!' She lifted her arm as if to strike out at the girl, but Holly was too quick for her. Dodging sideways, Holly ran through the open churchyard gate and along the path that led to the woods. Mrs Kent made a futile effort to grab at her, shouting, 'Come back here, Holly, this instant!'

The child paid no attention and, after a moment's hesitation, Jean Kent ran after her. The rector's wife was in reasonably good training, so that she was not far behind Holly as they reached the edge of the woods. Then suddenly her ankle turned on a broken branch and she was forced to stop.

Holly hadn't expected Mrs Kent to follow her with such determination. She ran on along the path, past the place where her father's body had been found, until she, too, was forced to an abrupt halt. A uniformed policeman—Sergeant Court, whom she knew well—leapt without warning from behind a tree, waving his arms in an effort to stop a small motor-bike approaching from the opposite direction. Holly screamed as the bike seemed to accelerate towards the Sergeant, who slid sideways into the undergrowth. The moped rider swerved to avoid Holly, hit a stump and skidded to the ground with his machine on top of him.

It was Thursday afternoon, and Superintendent Thorne's trap was working well.

The Superintendent and Sergeant Abbot had followed the motor-cyclist into the wood from the far road. They came up running as Court, having picked himself up, was starting to lift the motor-cycle. The three men converged on their victim. He was apparently unhurt, as he slowly got to his feet and took off his crash helmet.

'Why,' said Holly, 'it's Mr Wilson.'

Joe Wilson ignored her. He glared at Superintendent Thorne. 'What's all this?' he said. 'What in hell's name do you want? I've done nothing wrong.'

'At the very least you've been withholding evidence, Mr Wilson,' said Thorne. 'And that's no light matter in a murder enquiry. Is it, Sergeant?'

'No,' said Abbot. 'Very serious.'

Wilson wet his lips with a flickering tongue and his eyes darted from side to side as if he were contemplating flight. He swallowed hard. 'You—you don't understand,' he said. 'It's got nothing to do with the shooting.'

'Suppose you explain,' Thorne said.

'Yes. I—I'll have to. But not in front of her.' Wilson gestured at Holly. 'What I've got to say is—is private, like.'

'Quite,' said Thorne. 'Anyway, this is hardly a suitable place for an interview. Mr Wilson, I think you'd better accompany us to our headquarters at Kidlington. We've every facility there.'

'The formality of the Superintendent's words seemed to shock Wilson. 'No, no,' he said. 'Please. You don't understand. I've got to get home, and truly I've done nothing—' He stopped speaking. His eyes widened and his mouth dropped open. The three police officers swung round in the direction he was staring.

'It's only Mrs Kent,' Holly said calmly.

She was quite right. In spite of her twisted ankle, Jean Kent had continued to follow Holly, and now she came limping round a corner of the path. Wilson's evident surprise was a little excessive, thought the Superintendent fleetingly, as Mrs Kent confronted him, hands thrust deep in the pockets of her raspberry-coloured slacks.

'You must be Superintendent Thorne,' she declared aggressively. 'What's going on here? Has this wretched child been telling you more lies about me?'

'I don't tell lies,' Holly said.

'You said you told the Superintendent you saw me running out of the wood on Monday afternoon, and that's a flagrant untruth!'

Thorne sighed. Things seemed to be getting a little out of hand, but he couldn't resist the opportunity. 'You deny it, Mrs Kent?' he said.

'Of course I do. Categorically. And if you're not prepared to take my word against this—'

Joe Wilson interrupted her. He was far from articulate, but his meaning was plain, and his earlier excessive surprise was explained. 'I saw—I saw—' he said. 'That bright pink. She must have heard me coming and run. But I did see it—just a glimpse between the trees—that bright pink.'

Jean Kent rounded on him. 'What on earth are you talking about, Wilson?'

'I saw—' Wilson began again, but the Superintendent held up his hand to stop him. 'Ah yes, Mr Wilson, you were going to tell us what happened last Monday, but we agreed this wasn't the best place. And we certainly don't need to detain you, Mrs Kent, or Holly.'

He gave them each a thin smile, a false smile that wasn't intended to deceive. It served its purpose, however. Holly nodded her thanks and ran off at once. Jean Kent was slower but, as Thorne waited, she gave him a bitter glance, opened her mouth and shut it without speaking, shrugged and limped off.

'Now, Mr Wilson,' Thorne said.

Joe Wilson was no fool, and he'd had a moment to think. 'Superintendent, please! My sister-in-law will be expecting me at Mr Grayson's house. It's where I usually keep my bike. We—we could talk there. Mr Grayson's in London, I know. And—and it would be much better for me.'

Thorne was not an unkind man, and he already had an

inkling of what he was about to hear. 'All right,' he said.
'You lead the way. Sergeant Abbot and I will come with
you. We shan't need Sergeant Court's help any more.
Many thanks,' he added, as Court took the hint and
started back towards the road.

Wilson pushed his bike a few yards further along the
path, and stopped at a point where it straightened and,
Thorne noticed, the site of the murder was clearly in
view. Wilson suddenly lifted his machine over a fallen
tree-trunk on the right, and plunged with some difficulty
into what appeared to be a mass of undergrowth. Thorne
and Abbot followed and found themselves on the merest
of tracks. The procession continued for some minutes,
Wilson still carrying his bike, until they were halted by
the back of a wooden shed, with a light paling fence
stretching from it in each direction. There was no doubt
in Superintendent Thorne's mind that they had reached
the northern boundary of Grayson's garden.

Thorne and Abbot exchanged glances. They had both
seen signs of efforts to conceal the fact that the track was
in occasional use. What they were wondering was why the
officers who had searched the site had failed to bring
them to their attention. They shrugged mentally,
simultaneously realizing the effects of conditions after
Monday's storm. The searchers hadn't had the advantage
of being shown.

There was no immediately apparent opening in the
wooden wall that faced them, but it seemed that some of
the boards had been loosened. Wilson, after a little
fiddling, was able to push three of them aside, and lift his
bike through the hole into what turned out to be a rather
large, untidy garden shed.

'Does Mr Grayson know you keep your bike here?'
Thorne asked, once they were all inside.

'No, He's not much of a gardener and he doesn't come
in here. Even if he looked in he wouldn't see it. I keep it

covered with an old blanket.'

'But Mrs Wilson—your sister-in-law—she knows?'

'Yes. She knows everything,' Wilson said morosely. 'She'll be expecting me about now. There'll be a cup of tea ready.'

'Good!' said Thorne at once. 'I could do with one myself, and so could Sergeant Abbot. Lead the way.'

A few minutes later the three of them were sitting around the kitchen table with Mrs Wilson. The Superintendent was relaxed and very much at ease. Abbot tried to emulate him. But, with Mrs Wilson on the verge of tears and Joe Wilson staring vacantly into space, he found it difficult.

Superintendent Thorne said, 'Mr Wilson, we followed you to the village of Farringdale today, and we assume that's where you go twice a week. Suppose you tell us why, and what happened last Monday.'

Joe Wilson screwed up his mouth as if in pain; it clearly wasn't easy for him to speak frankly. Finally he said, 'Superintendent, I—I love my wife. She's a wonderful woman, sweet and brave, but—But I'm only forty and she's an invalid. She can't—not any more—be a—a real wife. Oh God! It seemed such a wonderful idea when I met Ruth again. I've known her—Ruth—Mrs Humble— since I was a boy. She's a widow now and we thought, if we were terribly careful, no one would ever find out. It wouldn't do no harm and—' Wilson buried his face in his hands.

'Joe's a good man,' Mrs Wilson said, 'and he's a good husband. You ask anyone, Superintendent. Ask Sergeant Abbot here. He does everything for that girl.'

'Please!' Thorne held up his hand, then absent-mindedly took a sip of tea. 'I'm not here to pass judgement on anyone's morals. Mr Wilson's activities in Farringdale aren't my business, unless—'

'You mean it won't become public? No one need know?'

Joe Wilson looked up, suddenly full of hope.

'I can't promise that,' Thorne said, and Wilson sagged again. 'What I was going to say, Mr Wilson, was that your affairs aren't my business, unless they're related to our enquiries. Now, let's get back to Monday. You rode off to Farringdale, and back again. When you rode into the wood on your return trip, what did you see? Who did you see? Peter Derwent?' Thorne was urgent now, no longer casual, and Abbot wondered at his superior's ability to vary the pace of an interrogation so effortlessly. 'Mr Wilson, it's a question of murder, you know,' Thorne added softly.

'I didn't kill him!' Wilson exclaimed at once. 'He was dead when I got there—' He stopped, looking from one police officer to the other.

Joe Wilson's story was quite simple, but it took some time to extract, largely because Wilson was ashamed of the part he'd played. In short, he hadn't heard the shot, but he might have caught a glimpse of the murderer. As he came to the straight part of the path, he'd seen the figure lying on the ground in its yellow oilskin. Leaving his moped, he'd run to it, turned back the hood for a moment, and immediately recognized Derwent. Derwent hadn't moved or spoken or looked at him. Then, glancing up, Wilson had seen a flash of deep pink disappearing among the dripping trees.

'Mrs Kent,' he said. 'It could have been. That's why I was so startled earlier when she came after Holly Derwent.'

'But you're not certain it was Mrs Kent?' Thorne pressed.

'No, though Holly said—' Wilson shook his head. 'No,' he repeated, 'I just caught a glimpse. It could have been anyone, man or woman. I've got a shirt that colour myself.'

Wilson was silent, and Thorne had to prompt him.

'Then? What did you do? Why didn't you go for help?'

'I came here as fast as I could—but there was no one in the kitchen.' It was an inadequate answer, as Wilson clearly realized.

'I was upstairs.' Mrs Wilson tried to help. 'The rain had come through one of the windows. I mopped it up and checked all round the house. I found Joe when I came down, and he told me what had happened. Then Mr Grayson came into the kitchen about something, and—I know we should have told him, but—' Now in difficulties herself, she looked desperately at her brother-in-law.

'I know,' said Thorne. 'If you had, the whole thing could have come out—the motor-bike, the visits to Mrs Humble—and Mrs Wilson, Mrs Joe Wilson, might have got to know. So you let Mr Derwent die, alone, in the wood.'

'I thought he—'

'Joe said he—'

They began together and stopped. Mrs Wilson started to cry. Joe Wilson said, 'I was going back. I swear I was. Just as soon as Mr Grayson left us I went out to the road. I meant to go along the path—to find Mr Derwent for the first time, like. It had stopped raining by then and I could have said I was going to Broadfields about something. But I saw Mr Kent—the Rector—go into the wood, and I knew he'd find him.'

'As indeed he did,' Thorne said. 'And incidentally, Mr Wilson, Mr Derwent was still alive when Mr Kent found him. He managed to utter a few words, and the last thing he said was your name.'

Joe Wilson was stunned. 'But he can't have. He didn't see me. He didn't know I was there. I swear he didn't.'

'So why should he mention you?'

'Why? I don't know. I swear I don't.'

The questioning continued, now intense, now more relaxed, but Joe Wilson stuck to his story and Mrs Wilson supported him. As Thorne and Abbot left the house, Abbot said, 'Did you believe them, sir?'

George Thorne looked blank. 'Someone's lying,' he said. 'Maybe more than one. But who? Your guess is as good as mine.'

CHAPTER 10

The funeral took place the following Monday, a week after Peter Derwent's death. Superintendent Thorne and Sergeant Abbot arrived at St Mary's church very early. Two choirboys were setting out printed orders of service. An unseen player was drawing mournful sounds from an organ. A woman, identified by Abbot as the wife of Alfred Meakin, a neighbouring farmer, was putting finishing touches to the flowers. And, surprisingly, the Reverend Simon Kent, in a long, black cassock, was picking up a collection of wilted wild daisies that seemed to have been strewn randomly on the polished oak coffin and around it. For a moment the Superintendent thought this must be part of some outlandish Cotswold custom, but then he came to his senses. 'I guess I know who scattered those,' he said to Abbot. 'That child Holly, I'll bet.'

The two officers chose their seats carefully, in a rear pew and on a side aisle. From here they had an excellent view of everyone entering the church, and as the congregation grew Abbot, who knew many of the people by sight, murmured brief descriptions.

The weather still hadn't broken and the day was hot and sultry. Most of the men wore light suits, the women summer dresses. Though the colours were pale, the general atmosphere was of festivity rather than mourning. This impression was enhanced by the arrival

of Jean Kent, who strode up the aisle in a deep pink
trouser suit, with a matching peaked cap.

'It seems to be her favourite colour,' Abbot whispered.

The Superintendent nodded without smiling. He had
just caught a strange, doubtful expression on Joe Wilson's
face as the publican saw Mrs Kent. Then Wilson turned
and muttered something to his sister-in-law. Thorne
wished he could have heard what it was.

By now the church was almost full. The Derwents were
naturally well known in the neighbourhood, and local
people were joined by pupils at the riding school with
their parents, and friends from Oxford or further afield.
As he saw many members of the congregation eyeing him
and Abbot inquisitively, Thorne wondered a little
cynically how many of them were there out of curiosity
because Peter Derwent had met a violent end. Then the
organ voluntary ceased, a solitary church bell began to
toll and the mutter of conversation gradually subsided.
The family was arriving.

Lorna came first with Richard, followed by the two
girls and Nina, escorted by Tim Railton. In dark clothes,
unsuitable for the weather, they looked hot and
uncomfortable. They walked down the aisle and took
their places in the front pew. The service commenced.

Simon Kent had given careful thought to his eulogy.
He would have liked it to be brief and simple, to appear
extemporaneous and from the heart. But he knew he
wasn't capable of such a performance, so he had
prepared careful notes, as he always did for his sermons.
He began by saying that Peter had been a good man, who
had given up a career he loved when it became necessary
for him to return to Broadfields, a good husband, a good
father and, as he himself could vouch, a good friend and
neighbour.

But here Simon Kent faltered, his gaze fixed on the
back of the church. Someone had come through the

porch and was standing in the arched entrance, outlined against the bright sunshine. He was a tall young man with dark hair and an unmistakable long, narrow face. Dressed in scarlet slacks and a white, open-necked shirt he looked as if he were a tourist who had wandered into the middle of a funeral by mistake.

In fact, John Derwent had been on his way to Broadfields. Confronted by a policeman directing traffic around the long line of parked cars outside the church, he had stuck his head out of the window of his rented car and asked what was happening. 'Funeral, sir,' the policeman said. 'Mr Derwent's, from up at the big house.'

'What?' John Derwent stared at him. 'You mean Peter Derwent's dead?'

'Yes, sir. Last Monday. He was found in the woods over there.' The officer looked at him curiously. 'Did you know him, sir?'

'I sure did. He was my cousin.' John Derwent hesitated. This scarcely seemed the right time or place for questions. 'Can I park somewhere?' he said.

Directed to the end of the row, he left his car and walked back to the church and up the path. After the bright sunlight it was dark in the interior of the church and he paused on the threshold to let his eyes adjust. He was aware that a speaker's voice had faltered as he appeared, and he sensed heads turning in his direction. By now he could see clearly, and a girl — a child whom he recognized as Holly — leapt up from her seat at the front of the church and screamed.

'Get out! Get out!' she cried. 'We don't want you here, John Derwent! It's not yours! It's—'

Her words were cut short as she was pulled down into her seat, a hand clasped over her mouth. 'No, Holly, no. You mustn't. It's not John's fault, darling.' Nina Langden held her firmly, rocking her till she felt the young body relax. 'It's all right, Holly.'

'It's not all right!' Clare whispered fiercely. 'How could you, Holly? How could you? Poor John. What will he think of us?' Her face was red with anger.

Tim Railton leant across Nina. 'Shut up!' he said angrily. 'Both of you. You're in church. This is your father's funeral.'

But others too had forgotten the occasion. The congregation whispered and shuffled. Simon Kent's carefully prepared address had ended in confusion as he knocked his notes to the floor of the pulpit, and tried desperately to rearrange them. John Derwent fled.

Only the organist showed any presence of mind. She began to play 'Abide with me'. Someone in the church started to sing, and the choir and the rest of the congregation joined in raggedly. A few rows in front of Thorne and Abbot, Trevor Grayson stood and added a fine baritone to the hymn. The incident was over.

Five minutes later, preceded by the coffin and the family, everyone was filing from the church. The Derwents and their closer friends gathered by the open grave. Others, not invited to return to Broadfields afterwards, dispersed, now talking more freely.

Astounded and shocked by Holly's virulent attack, John Derwent had gone back to his car. He sat behind the wheel and wondered what he should do. He had tried to call Lorna three or four times in the past week, but the number had always been busy. In the end, he had written her a note saying when he would be arriving in Colombury. He'd expected to be made welcome. The last thing he'd anticipated was that he would arrive in the middle of Peter's funeral and be sworn at in public by his youngest English cousin.

He saw that people were beginning to leave the church, so he hastily started the engine and drove down the road to Colombury. What he needed, he decided, was a drink and some lunch. He'd go up to Broadfields during the afternoon when, with any luck, the Derwents would be alone. He remembered the Windrush Arms from his previous visit, and parked outside. In the bar, he ordered a gin and tonic. He drank half standing up then took his glass to a seat by a window.

Lost in thought, he was startled when two men came to his table and, without invitation, sat down opposite him. 'Mr Derwent? Mr John Derwent?' one of them enquired.

'That's right,' he agreed, unsmiling. 'And who are you?'

'I'm Detective-Superintendent Thorne of the Thames Valley Police, and this is Detective-Sergeant Abbot.' Thorne produced his warrant card. 'I wonder if you'd mind answering a few questions.'

'Like what?'

'Well, to start with, would you tell us where you were last Monday afternoon — just a week ago.'

John Derwent was twenty-nine, and highly intelligent. What was more, he was a lawyer, and lectured at the Harvard Law School. He wasn't prepared to be bullied by a couple of British cops. So he took his time before answering.

'Last Monday?' he said finally. 'In the afternoon I was driving from Oxford to Stratford-on-Avon. I had a ticket for *As You Like It* that night. Why?'

'We're investigating a death, sir — the death of Mr Peter Derwent, which occurred at about that time. It's a mere formality, naturally, but you appear to have been in the neighbourhood at the time, and you stand to gain by the death, so we'd be failing in our duty if we didn't —' Superintendent Thorne let his words trail into silence.

'I see,' said John Derwent levelly. 'I take it the death was suspicious.'

'Mr Derwent was murdered, sir, shot in the back in the woods near his home. I understand that on his death you became the owner of the Derwent home and property.'

There was a pause, while Thorne sat waiting
impassively. At last John Derwent said, 'Yes, I believe
that's so. What else do you want to know?'

To Sergeant Abbot's frustration, the Superintendent
seemed to want to know very little. He made a fairly
casual attempt to establish more precisely John Derwent's
whereabouts at the time of the murder, and then
suggested abruptly that Richard Derwent and the
immediate family, especially the widow, had been rather
hardly done by. John politely agreed that it was
unfortunate for them that his own father had bought
Broadfields, but volunteered no more.

'A cool character,' Superintendent Thorne said when
John Derwent had left them in search of the dining-room.
'He certainly doesn't give much away.'

'He could have taken in Colombury on his way from
Oxford to Stratford,' Abbot said eagerly. 'It's readily
possible—'

'And he had a .22 rifle in the car with him, of course.'
Thorne was sarcastic. 'Because he knew he'd find Peter
Derwent walking through those damned woods in a storm
at just the right moment. Don't build castles in the air,
Abbot.' The Superintendent shook his head in disgust.
'It's no good, you know. It simply doesn't add up.'

As he drove to Broadfields after a lunch he'd scarcely
touched, John Derwent might superficially have seemed a
cool character. Inwardly, however, he had rarely felt
more nervous.

But when he reached the house his fears weren't
realized. His note warning them of his plans hadn't yet
been delivered, but his room was ready. He was greeted
affectionately and made welcome. With the sole
exception of a subdued Holly, everyone seemed genuinely
delighted at his arrival. And only the occasional oblique

reference was made to his ownership of Broadfields.

Lorna, having said how glad she was to see him, added, 'We all are. Please forgive Holly. She didn't mean to be horrid.'

And a little later, as he was going, Tim Railton said, 'You and I must get together soon, John, but there's no hurry for a day or two.'

It wasn't until after supper, when he was alone with Clare in the stables, that John Derwent broached the subject himself. He put his hand on her arm, and said, 'Clare, please don't feel bitter about Broadfields.'

'I don't, John,' she said at once. 'Broadfields would have been Richard's anyway, not mine.' John Derwent tried to pull her towards him, but she turned away, wrinkling her forehead. 'I think Aunt Nina's calling,' she said. 'I must go.'

Again John took her arm in an effort to stop her. 'Please Clare, just one minute. You know how terribly important you are to me.'

Clare flushed and shook her head. But she smiled. 'Would you like to go riding early tomorrow?' she said. 'Glory was lame last week, but she's fine again now.'

John looked at her for a long moment. 'I'd like nothing more,' he said. And he thought the day was ending better than he could have hoped.

CHAPTER 11

For Tim Railton the day of Peter Derwent's funeral had been a mixture of grief and irritation. He wasn't sure what had been worst — Holly's outburst, Nina's terrifying self-control, or Lorna, who had so retreated within herself that he had found it impossible to make real contact with her. It had been a day of memories and regrets.

Thankful it was over, but worried by what was to come, he drove the following morning to his office, parked in the courtyard and walked along the High Street to the bank. He had an appointment with Brian Curtis, the manager, to discuss Peter Derwent's financial affairs.

The two men were old friends. They shook hands. 'Coffee?' Curtis said. 'I always have a cup before I start work in the morning.'

'Thanks.' Railton wasn't deceived by the casual approach. He had considerable respect for the bank manager's competence, and he had already noted the single file on the otherwise empty desk. 'Had a good holiday?'

'Very good, thank you.' Curtis waited until his secretary had poured the coffee and left the room. 'But I came back to bad news, Tim. I was truly sorry to hear about Peter Derwent. He was a pleasant chap. I can't imagine why anyone should want — Are the police making any progress?'

'Not as far as I know. There's a detective-superintendent and a sergeant from Kidlington asking a lot of questions around the town, but they've certainly not told me if they're on to anything. I should have thought they'd have been into the bank by now, seeing your deputy. If they haven't, they decided to wait for your return, like me.' Railton sipped his coffee. 'Brian, you must be very busy after being away, and I don't want to keep you unnecessarily. But you know I'm Peter's executor, and there do seem to be one or two problems.'

'The size of his overdraft, for instance.' Curtis opened the file and pushed a piece of paper across the desk. 'Here's how the account stands as of now.'

Railton glanced at the figure and sighed. 'Did you always let him run such a large overdraft?'

'It varied. This was the absolute maximum we'd allow him. But sometimes it was smaller. He hadn't got that bad a track record. A few years ago he paid off the whole lot—he said something about a killing on the Stock Exchange—but it's grown steadily again since then.'

'That would be about five years ago? When he was suddenly flourishing, I mean?'

'Yes, that's right.'

When he sold Broadfields, Railton thought. At least I know where some of the money he got from old Daniel went. 'Was he much in the red at that time, Brian—before the sudden affluence?'

'Up to his neck, though that was a fairly recent state at the time. Let me see.' Curtis shuffled through the papers in front of him. 'Yes. Before then he'd not been doing too badly. I'd guess he got in a hole somehow, took a gamble that paid off and managed to climb out—at least temporarily. That's why we were prepared to carry him again. After all, he's a big landowner, and the record's not that bad, as I said.'

'I see,' said Railton slowly. From the bank's point of view the position wasn't disastrous, but Curtis didn't know the whole story, and he wasn't prepared to enlighten him, not yet. Instead, Railton opened his briefcase and took out the file of bank statements he'd found in Peter Derwent's office. 'There's one other point, Brian—this Standing Order for two hundred pounds a month. Can you give me the details? I'll have to decide what to do about it?'

'Of course,' said Curtis readily. 'Here we are. Payable at the beginning of each month to the account of Arthur William Derwent at our Lower Regent Street branch in London. Account number—'

But Tim Railton was no longer listening. Peter had never mentioned an Arthur William Derwent. He was sure of that. Yet, for the last four and a half years, from a time soon after he'd been forced to sell Broadfields, Peter had been paying this man an income—not large, but steady. Why?

'—I'll get my secretary to type out the details for you. Do you want me to make any enquiries in London?'

Railton thought for a moment. 'No,' he said, 'I'll do it myself. You can give me a letter of introduction to the manager there, though.' Then he added. 'It would have helped the overdraft if there hadn't been this drain on the account, wouldn't it, Brian?'

'Of course it would. In fact, I pointed that out to Peter once, but he wouldn't listen. He said he couldn't possibly stop the payments.' The bank manager's expression was a little disbelieving. 'Evidently Arthur Derwent's pretty well penniless, and this was practically his only source of income.' Curtis shrugged. 'Personally I thought Peter's charity should have started nearer home.'

Tim Railton nodded. It was a sentiment with which he thoroughly agreed. Peter was a generous man and this Arthur William was presumably a relation, but the relationship couldn't have been very close or he would surely have heard the name. Or Nina would—

As soon as he reached his own office Railton phoned Broadfields and asked for Nina. He told her he'd come across the name of Arthur William Derwent in Peter's papers. Did she know who he was?

'No,' said Nina at once. 'At least, I don't think so. Let me try to remember. Of my generation there were only Gerald and me. Our father had an elder sister who never married—and anyway, if she had, her children wouldn't have been Derwents. There were a couple of younger brothers who were both killed—without issue, as they say—in the 'fourteen-'eighteen war. Neither was called Arthur. And then of course there was a much younger half-brother—my grandfather married twice. He—the half-brother—was the one that emigrated to the States.'

'That would be John's—grandfather?'

'Yes. I know it's a bit odd, because Richard and John

are approximate contemporaries. But the American branch skipped a generation. Perhaps it's a pity we didn't; then maybe we'd have been as successful as they were—moneywise and otherwise.'

Tim Railton laughed. He liked Nina's clarity and her acerbic sense of humour. But she hadn't helped with the problem of Arthur William. It was extremely unlikely that the recipient of Peter Derwent's charity had come from the American branch of the family. If so, he'd have done better to appeal to old Daniel, or John, rather than to the impoverished Peter.

'—Shall I get John to ring you?' Nina was saying. 'He's out at the moment, riding with Clare. Doubtless she'll come back all starry-eyed. I only hope . . . He's ten years older than she is, and far more experienced, I'm sure.'

'My dear Nina!' Tim Railton laughed again. 'Clare can take care of herself. Don't worry about them. Ask John to give me a ring if he's ever heard of an Arthur William, will you? Otherwise, not to bother.'

'Yes, I will, Tim. Bless you.'

Railton sighed as he put down the receiver. There was nothing for it but a trip to London. It was a nuisance when he was so damned busy, but there was no way the enquiries could be made on the phone. He flicked on his intercom and asked Mrs Kirby to make an appointment for him with the Regent Street bank manager as soon as possible.

'Say it's urgent,' he said. 'Tell him it concerns an estate.'

He sat back in his chair and wondered if the matter really was that urgent. Even if he was right and Peter Derwent had been paying blackmail rather than dispensing charity to some indigent relative, there was no way he could see that the blackmail tied in with Peter's death. There were no signs that Peter intended to cease the payments, and no one was stupid enough to kill a goose while it was laying golden eggs.

Tim Railton was still pondering the matter when his secretary returned to say that the bank manager could see him before lunch the following day. He and Mrs Kirby then spent the next hour rearranging his appointments so that he could spend Wednesday in London.

In the meantime, Trevor Grayson was on his way to Broadfields. Though he'd felt slightly averse to walking through the woods since Peter Derwent's death, nevertheless he went that way. He was anxious to avoid any impression of a formal call; he'd been out for a stroll and was taking the opportunity to drop in, as any friend of the family might. In fact, he had a genuine and personal reason for visiting the Derwents.

The reason was simple. He wanted to establish, as far as he could, the Derwents' financial situation. An astute man, he had surmised from what he knew of Peter Derwent's admitted difficulties, from rumours stirring in Colombury, even from young Holly's outburst at the funeral, that the Derwent family might be unable in the future to keep up what remained of the Broadfields estate.

After almost five years Grayson was well established in the neighbourhood, largely thanks, he was aware, to his original acceptance by the Derwents as an acquaintance—if not a friend—of the late Michael Derwent, Peter's brother. He had no wish to move, nor to see the Derwent family leave Broadfields. He hated to think what might happen if the estate were broken up: speculative building, a hotel—the possibilities were endless. No, the present situation suited him very well, and he needed forewarning of any impending changes.

As he emerged from the woods Grayson was sweating. It was yet another hot, sticky morning, the sky dark and lowering, still threatening a storm. A strange summer, he thought, as he knocked on the open back door, and not a happy one.

'Come in!' Lorna had seen Grayson from the window, and was able to sound more welcoming than she felt. Usually, when he called, he came to the front door and rang the bell; she wondered what had happened to make him change his habit. 'You're just in time for some iced coffee, Trevor,' she said as he appeared in the kitchen. 'Instant, I'm afraid.'

'I'm not intruding?' Grayson turned his heavy face from Lorna, busy at the sink, to Nina, who was sitting at the table, shelling peas. The two women shook their heads. 'Good. I was out for a walk, and I hoped you wouldn't mind if I looked in. All alone, are you? Where's the rest of the family?'

Lorna thought the question somewhat abrupt, but she answered readily enough. 'Clare's giving Betty Meakin— the farmer's daughter—a dressage lesson. John—our American cousin—he's in the garden somewhere.'

'And Richard,' Nina added, 'has gone to Oxford to see his old tutor about a grant.'

'A grant?' Grayson asked quickly.

Lorna frowned at Nina, but Nina continued. 'Yes, he's got his degree, but he still has to take his Law Society exams. And as there'll be precious little money to go round after Peter's estate is settled, he's hoping—'

'Nina!' Lorna protested. 'Trevor's not interested in our personal affairs.' Hurriedly she poured out coffee and gave each of them a mug. 'Sugar, Trevor?'

'Er—no, thanks.' Grayson appeared embarrassed. In fact, he was trying to think of a way to change the subject without totally abandoning it. Finally, he said, 'Clare seems to be making a go of the stables. I often see her pupils passing. You know, I used to ride a lot in Africa, and I've often thought of taking it up again. I suppose Clare wouldn't consider selling me that mare of hers—what does she call her: something Glory?'

'Vain Glory,' Lorna said, surprised. 'You'll have to ask her, Trevor.'

'I'd keep her at the stables, of course.'

Lorna smiled politely. Nina finished shelling the peas and regarded her handiwork. 'That won't be enough,' she said. 'I'll have to pick some more—and get some mint.' She drank the rest of her coffee and collected a basket. 'Goodbye for now, Trevor.'

Lorna waited a moment in the expectation that Grayson would take the implied hint, but he showed no sign of leaving so she said, 'I must make a pudding for tonight. We can't live on ice-cream and fruit, even in this weather. You'll forgive me, Trevor, if I get on with my chores?'

'Of course,' Grayson said.

He seemed to be deep in thought, his face expressionless. Lorna glanced at him doubtfully, then began to collect her ingredients, moving busily around the kitchen. But still Trevor Grayson continued to sit.

To break the lengthening silence, Lorna remarked, 'I've had so many letters from people who knew Peter, and they're still coming. I don't know when I'll find time to answer them all.'

Her words seemed to galvanize Trevor Grayson. 'I'm not surprised. Peter had a lot of friends. I count myself among them. Which is why, Lorna, though I'm far from being a rich man, I'd gladly offer you any help I could to keep up Broadfields. I hope I haven't offended you—'

'My dear Trevor!' Lorna came round the table and impulsively took both his hands. 'How kind of you! How very kind!'

'What else could I say?' she demanded later when Trevor Grayson had gone and Nina had returned with her basket of vegetables. 'I was touched, overwhelmed.'

'Of course you were. Who wouldn't be? Good for

Trevor!' Nina wiped the perspiration from her upper lip and sat down heavily. 'God, it's hot and stuffy,' she said. 'If we're going to have a storm I wish we'd get it over.'

Trevor Grayson had left Broadfields well satisfied with his morning's effort. At least he'd acquired a good idea of the situation. Richard was in need of a grant. The suggestion that Clare might sell her favourite horse hadn't met with a firm refusal. Even his offer to help Lorna financially hadn't been turned down immediately or indignantly. All this added up to the probability that the Derwents were more or less broke. Grayson wondered if he should await developments, or cut his losses and put his house on the market at once.

He'd miss the place, he thought, as he came to the first trees and paused to mop his brow. Like Nina, he wished the storm would break. This sort of weather was unnatural in England and made him feel disturbed, expectant, even nervous. Shaking his head, he plunged into the wood.

He was approaching the place where Peter Derwent's body had been found when he heard the crackle of twigs and a rustle of leaves behind him. 'Mr Grayson,' a voice said quite quietly, and he swung round. Momentarily he was startled. But he'd already begun to relax, his mouth stretching into a smile of recognition, when he saw the rifle.

'No!' he cried. 'No! Don't —'

The bullet hit him beside the breastbone. Unlike Peter Derwent, he died almost at once, with very little blood and no last words. And again unlike Peter Derwent, he was not allowed to lie where he had fallen. Instead, the killer seized him under the armpits and with great difficulty, for he was a heavy man, pulled him off the path into the undergrowth and then rapidly scuffed over obvious traces of his passage. Two minutes later no one passing casually along the path would have noticed any signs of the incident.

Mrs Wilson's first reaction when her employer failed to come home for lunch was annoyance. He might have phoned, she thought. But it was a cold meal, and she shrugged off her irritation.

In the afternoon she called at the Grey Dove to visit her invalid sister-in-law, but she was back at the cottage in time to prepare tea. Mr Grayson still hadn't returned. By five o'clock she was beginning to worry; it was very unlike him to be away for so long without warning her.

She phoned Broadfields at about a quarter to seven. Yes, Mr Grayson had been there in the morning, but he had left well before lunch. Richard and John volunteered to walk through the wood just in case, as Richard said, he'd tripped and broken an ankle or something. The clouds were gathering as they set out and, busy talking, they passed the place where Grayson had been shot, and noticed nothing untoward.

At seven-thirty, not long after Richard and John returned to Broadfields, the storm finally broke. The sky was split by jagged lightning. Thunder rolled around the hills. The rains descended and a fierce wind lifted off tiles and brought down chimney pots and the occasional telephone pole. When Mrs Wilson tried to phone the police as the storm passed over, she found that her line was dead.

Thus is was not until the next morning that, after a sleepless night, Mrs Wilson hurried to the Grey Dove. From there, she was able to report Trevor Grayson's disappearance to Sergeant Court at the Colombury police station.

CHAPTER 12

At the Kidlington headquarters, Detective-Superintendent Thorne glared across his desk at Sergeant Abbot. 'Disappeared?' he demanded furiously. 'What do you mean—disappeared? Into thin air?'

Abbot, feeling like a delinquent schoolboy, did his best to explain. 'They've just been on from Colombury, sir. Apparently Grayson left Broadfields some time around noon yesterday and he's not been seen since. His housekeeper missed him last night, but the weather stopped her reporting it till this morning.'

'He's in those damned woods, I'll bet. What's Colombury doing about it?'

'They're searching the woods now, sir. They need some extra men.'

'To trample all over the bloody place again, I suppose.' Thorne stroked his moustache hard.

Abbot remained silent, and the telephone rang. The Superintendent seized it. 'Thorne,' he said, and listened. 'Okay,' he said finally. 'Now, I want the whole wood cordoned off immediately. Yes, all of it. You say Dr Band's seen him. Fine. No one, but no one else, is to go in, except one man by the body. Do nothing till I get there. Understood? Right.'

He slammed down the receiver, and stared at Abbot. 'Well, you heard. They've found him. Looks as if he was shot close by where Derwent was killed, but dragged off the path. No weapon found yet. Get a team down there double quick, but tell them to be careful not to disturb the ground. We'll go over that later with a fine-tooth comb. No half measures this time. And see the pathologist gets there right away . . .'

/

Superintendent Thorne continued to issue orders. Fifteen minutes later he and Abbot were on their way to Colombury, Abbot driving fast, Thorne slumped in the seat beside him. The storm had completely cleared, and the air was cool and fresh. Abbot began to feel more cheerful.

'At least we can cross Grayson off the list, sir,' he ventured.

Thorne grunted. 'As the killer—if there's no question of suicide. But he's involved somehow, I'm sure.' He stopped, and then added, 'I wish I knew what he and Derwent were really quarrelling about last week.'

The Superintendent lapsed into silence once more, and Abbot concentrated on the road. Sergeant Court was waiting for them where the path met the road. Already broad white tapes stretched among the trees, and police notices were in evidence. Thorne nodded his head in approval.

'We'll have a quick look at the body,' he said to Court. 'Then the experts can take over. They'll be here any minute.' He looked with disgust at the still-dripping trees and the rain-soaked ground as they started into the wood. 'Even the weather's against us. I take it Grayson was lying out here all through last night's downpour. What did Dr Band have to say, Court?'

'He could only give a preliminary estimate, sir, but he put the time of death at between twelve and twenty-four hours ago. He said it looked as if Grayson was killed by the same calibre bullet as Derwent.' Court sighed. 'Here we are, sir.'

A police constable, standing beside the path, saluted. Sergeant Court pushed his way carefully into the undergrowth and lifted the tarpaulin that covered Trevor Grayson's body.

'We had to clear things a bit, sir, so that the doctor could get to him. But he was pretty well hidden when we found him, though quite close to the path. I think the storm helped to hide him.'

Thorne nodded. His examination of the scene was brief. The reports of police surgeon, pathologist and the team would fill in the picture later. Meanwhile, it was vital to interview everyone who might help while events were still clear in their minds. He waited only to give more precise instructions to the officers from Kidlington who had by now reached the wood, before setting off on a round of calls.

'Broadfields, Abbot,' he said purposefully. 'Maybe we'll be first with the news.'

But the postman had beaten them to it, and any element of surprise was lost. Nevertheless, the Broadfields household seemed genuinely shocked. Nina summed up their feelings. 'It's appalling!' she said. 'Peter, then Trevor—and both so meaningless. It's as if a madman were at work. Who'll be next?'

'There won't be a next, Mrs Langden, not if I can help it.' Thorne ignored the doubtful glance she gave him. 'And not if you'll cooperate. We've got to establish exactly what Mr Grayson did yesterday. Now, he was here in the morning. Is that right?'

The Derwents were gathered in the sitting-room. Only John and Clare, out hacking with some pupils, were missing, and they arrived before the detectives had completed their interview. Between them they managed to produce a fairly clear picture of Grayson's movements and their own.

'He left here at ten past twelve,' Lorna said. 'I looked at the clock because I was thinking about lunch. I was alone when he went. Mrs Langden had gone into the garden a few minutes earlier to pick some more vegetables for dinner.'

Nina shook her head. 'I didn't see him from the kitchen garden. I couldn't. It's walled in.'

'But I did,' Clare said. 'I was coming back to the stables with Betty Meakin. Her dressage lesson ended at twelve, so it would have been about a quarter past. We saw him going along the path to the woods.'

'Good. That's fine as far as it goes. Did anyone else see him? Or hear a shot, or anything that could have been a shot?' Thorne looked expectantly round the room, but Richard hadn't returned from Oxford until after four and John, bored with dressage, had been reading in the garden, seen no one and heard nothing. 'What about you, Holly?' Thorne asked.

Holly regarded him appraisingly. 'I was helping Aunt Nina pick peas,' she said. 'I might have heard a shot, but it could have been a car back-firing or anything. Before that I was in the churchyard, looking at my Dad's grave. I don't think either Mr or Mrs Kent were at the rectory.'

'Turn left,' ordered Thorne, as the car slowed at the end of Broadfields drive. 'Let's go and have another word with old Mrs Daley.'

Mrs Daley was delighted to welcome them. She had not yet heard of Grayson's death, and Thorne was forced to tell her about it and then to parry her questions. When he was able to ask some of his own, however, her response was disappointing. She'd not been too well yesterday, and had stayed in bed until the district nurse called, so her vantage-point had been vacant at the relevant times.

'I'm sorry,' she said. 'I never even saw poor Mr Grayson. If only I'd known—'

Thorne avoided Abbot's eye. 'Never mind, Mrs Daley,' he said quickly. 'You were a great help to us last time.'

'About that chap on the little motor-bike, you mean. I didn't see him last Monday afternoon. He must have given it a miss. But the pink woman was there again yesterday.'

'Pink woman? There again?' Thorne exclaimed.

'Wearing one of those trouser suits. Bright pink, it is. My daughter-in-law saw her too. Her name's Mrs Kent, my daughter-in-law says. She's the parson's wife from the church up by Broadfields. Me, I don't hold with—'

It needed more prompting before the rest of the story became clear. Mrs Kent had been seen 'hovering'—Mrs Daley's word—where the main path through the woods reached the road. Mrs Daley was being helped to get up and dress, so it must have been about twelve o'clock. Naturally, Mrs Daley hadn't been watching out of the window all the time, and she couldn't say whether Mrs Kent had actually entered the woods or not.

'You said *again*, Mrs Daley?' Thorne's voice was gentle. 'You've seen the pink woman there before?'

'Yes, of course. The afternoon Mr Derwent died. Funny, wasn't it?'

Bill Abbot took a deep breath and released it slowly. Thorne, stroking his moustache, appeared unmoved, and the Sergeant wondered at his superior's apparent imperturbability. But suddenly the Superintendent thrust his face forward so that it was close to the old woman's.

'You never told us that the last time we were here, Mrs Daley,' he said. 'Why not?'

'You never asked me.' Mrs Daley wasn't one to be bullied or intimidated. She looked her indignation, then relented. 'To be honest, I just didn't think it mattered, not till today when I saw her again in the same place.'

'The first time—last week—did you see her go into the woods?'

'Yes, I did. She was standing near the road, just like today. Then Mr Derwent came out of Mr Grayson's house, and she dodged back into the trees.'

Thorne smiled thinly. 'Was she carrying anything?' he asked casually.

'Not this morning. About the other day, I wouldn't like to say. The rain was teeming down. I could easily have

missed her altogether if it hadn't been for that pink
outfit.'

There were more questions, but old Mrs Daley stood by
what she'd said, and the story was confirmed in part by
her daughter-in-law. 'Not a bad witness, not bad at all,
considering,' the Superintendent said as he and Abbot
were returning to their car. 'She may wander off the point
occasionally, but she doesn't invent things. What she says,
she believes. Let's go and call on Mrs Kent right now.'

Mrs Kent had been shopping in Colombury and was
about to unload her groceries from the boot of the car
when Thorne and Abbot arrived. She was still dressed in
a trouser suit, but today's was bright yellow. She was not
pleased to see them.

'And what do you want?' she demanded curtly. 'If it's
about Trevor Grayson, I know nothing. I've not set eyes
on him since Peter Derwent's funeral.'

'All the same, Mrs Kent, we think you may be able to
help us,' said Thorne placatingly. 'There are one or two
points—'

'Then you'll have to wait till I've got this lot inside.'

'Perhaps I—' Abbot began tentatively and, at a nod
from Thorne, helped to carry the boxes and bags through
to the kitchen.

Somewhat mollified by this unexpected assistance, Mrs
Kent invited them into her sitting-room. Thorne looked
around with interest. The Kents were lucky in that the
old, over-large and draughty Victorian rectory had been
replaced with a modern structure some years ago, but
surely only Mrs Kent's inherited money could have been
responsible for its interior. The Superintendent found
himself contrasting the relatively luxurious furnishings
with the fading shabbiness of Broadfields.

He turned to the Rector's wife, and began his
questions. Mrs Kent admitted she might have been seen

at the entrance to the woods the previous morning. She had walked through from the rectory, hesitated about going back the same way, and finally decided to return by the road. She had seen no one, and couldn't remember hearing a shot. She denied, and continued to deny, that she had been in the woods on the day Peter Derwent had been killed.

'Three to one,' Abbot remarked as they left the rectory. 'Mrs Daley, Joe Wilson and young Holly all claim they saw her.'

'But no one's seen her — or anyone else — in the right place at the right time, and with a rifle,' Thorne said sourly. 'What we need is the wretched weapon. If they don't find it in the woods, we'll have to spread the net wider. Meanwhile, let's get along to Mrs Wilson.'

'What about going to the Meakins' place first, sir? Their farm's just up the road.'

The Superintendent looked at his watch speculatively. Duty won. They'd have to fit in both interviews before lunch, and if necessary eat late. 'Right,' he said. 'Let it be Betty Meakin.'

The Meakins' farm looked prosperous. The house had been newly painted. The drive was well kept, the outbuildings neat and clean. The station wagon and the bright red Mini outside the front door were nearly new. But the reception accorded the two police officers didn't match this air of quiet well-being. Tom Meakin was even more aggressive than Mrs Kent.

'Police?' he said. 'Already? I was expecting your lot ever since I heard the glad news, but not so soon, I must admit. People been talking, have they?'

'You know how it is, Mr Meakin,' Thorne said vaguely. He hadn't the faintest idea what the farmer meant. 'People always talk.'

'And you've come to check up on the gossip? Well, I'll

tell you before you ask. It wasn't me that wasted Grayson, and I don't know who did. But whoever it was, I give him full marks. And I hope he gets away with it. Is that plain enough?'

Tom Meakin stood in his doorway, his eyes bright with malice, challenging Thorne. The Superintendent regarded him coldly. 'And that applies to Mr Derwent's murder too, does it, Mr Meakin?'

'Oh no,' Meakin said at once. 'No, it doesn't apply to Peter Derwent. I'm sorry about him, truly sorry. He didn't have a clue about running his place properly — or profitably — but he was a good man. He didn't go dashing round the lanes at sixty miles an hour killing valuable dogs.'

'Ah,' said Thorne. At last things were becoming a little clearer. 'Mr Grayson killed your dog.'

'I'll say he did! My Lindy. As beautiful and clever a collie as ever there was. If I'd had my way, I'd have —'

Meakin's tirade continued, much of it directed against the police, who had failed to collect sufficient evidence to send Grayson down for ten years . . . Thorne listened woodenly, then fired a succession of questions at the farmer. In the end, a somewhat chastened Meakin had to admit he owned a .22 sporting rifle, and had no alibi for either of the killings.

It was at this point that Thorne announced that they had really come to interview Meakin's daughter. The farmer's immediate reaction was surprise, but after a moment's hesitation he turned on his heel and called 'Betty' into the house behind him. The Superintendent had been visualizing another small girl, not unlike Holly Derwent. Instead, when she emerged, Miss Meakin turned out to be eighteen, a very well-developed and self-possessed young lady, and the owner of the red Mini.

Meakin showed no signs of inviting the police officers into his house, but Thorne had no objection to conducting his enquiries outdoors in the bright sunshine. In fact, Betty Meakin quickly confirmed what Clare Derwent had said. The two girls had seen Grayson going towards the wood at about twelve-fifteen. Betty had then collected her car from its parking place by the stables, and driven home, down Broadfields drive and past the Grey Dove at the 'Y' junction. She hadn't noticed anyone on foot, but she had heard a shot as she was approaching the rectory. It was a hot day, the Mini's windows were wide open, and she had no doubt it was a shot. She had once seen Mrs Kent bring down a rook, and she'd thought that this was probably a repeat performance.

From the Meakins' farm Thorne and Abbot at last made their way to Grayson's cottage to call on Mrs Wilson. She had already heard the tragic news, that her employer had been found dead in the woods—shot, just like Mr Derwent. 'Joe, my brother-in-law, came in and told me,' she said.

To Thorne's relief she seemed quite composed, even pleased to see someone in authority and seek his support. 'I wasn't sure what was the right thing to do,' she went on. 'I know Mr Grayson's got no relations—none close, that is. So in the end I phoned his solicitor.'

'Quite right,' said Thorne. 'And who was he?' he asked, thinking he knew the answer.

'Mr Railton of Railton, Mercer and Grey in Colombury, I think. Anyway, I spoke to a Mrs Kirby—Mr Railton's secretary, she said she was. She told me Mr Railton was in London today, but she promised to tell him as soon as he gets back.'

The Superintendent bowed his head in approval of Mrs Wilson's action. Then he took her, slowly and carefully, through the events of the previous day. When nothing new emerged, he reverted to the day of Peter Derwent's death.

'You said Mr Grayson and Mr Derwent had words,' he prompted. 'Could you amplify that—tell us any more about it?'

'No, not really. I know it was Mr Derwent who was angry. Mr Grayson was the calm one. I did hear Mr Derwent say something about money and something about some land. But that's all, Superintendent. I don't know what else. I'm sorry.'

'That's all right, Mrs Wilson. And Mr Derwent left soon afterwards?'

'Well, the storm started. There was a great clap of thunder and it began to pour. I ran round making sure all the windows were shut. When I went into the sitting-room Mr Grayson suggested an early tea, but Mr Derwent wasn't having any. He insisted on leaving.' She broke off and looked up at Thorne in some exasperation. 'But I've told you all this before.'

Thorne merely smiled, and Mrs Wilson was forced to continue. 'Foolish man—Mr Derwent, I mean. It was simply teeming down. He should have waited, but he wouldn't. He was so angry I think he'd have gone straight off as he was—without any coat or anything. At least we persuaded him to take Mr Grayson's oilskin—his old yellow slicker, as Mr Grayson called it.'

There was an inarticulate sound from Bill Abbot, and the Superintendent glared at him. Five minutes later, as they were heading towards the Windrush Arms and a late lunch, the Sergeant said miserably, 'Wouldn't you know, sir? Why in God's name didn't anyone say before that Derwent was wearing Grayson's oilskin?'

'Because it didn't seem important to them, I suppose. Or because we didn't ask the right questions.' Superintendent Thorne sounded quite calm, even triumphant. 'But now we know. We're getting somewhere, Abbot, slowly but surely. A most productive morning,' he added with satisfaction. 'Most productive.'

CHAPTER 13

Tim Railton found that Wednesday morning equally productive. He left home early and drove himself to London, avoiding the worst of the commuter traffic. He spent some time shopping, and eventually made his way to Lower Regent Street.

The main West End office of the bank was a far cry from its Colombury branch. An enquiry for Mr Meade, the senior manager, produced a uniformed messenger who escorted him to a waiting-room complete with deep leather chairs and large potted plants. An efficient-looking secretary took his letter of introduction, and Meade himself came out of his inner sanctum to welcome his visitor. He offered his hand, and ushered Railton through the door.

'A pleasure to meet you, Mr Railton,' he said. 'I hope we can be of service. Let's sit over there.' He indicated three or four chairs grouped around a coffee table to one side of the large office. 'I hate discussions across a desk, don't you? You'll have some coffee?'

Railton, who'd had coffee during his shopping, would have refused, but the secretary was already bringing in a tray. Mr Meade had not intended a question. Railton sat, accepted coffee and biscuits and considered his host, waiting for a lead. It was not long in coming.

Meade looked at his watch and said, 'Now, Mr Railton, what can we do for you? All I know at the moment is that the matter concerns an estate of which you're the executor. Our Colombury manager's letter indicates that the deceased was a client of his, but doesn't give his name. I assume there's a problem, but I don't see where we come in.'

'Not really a problem,' said Railton. 'At least, I hope not.' He opened his briefcase. 'Perhaps you'd glance through this copy of the will? Of course, we've not got probate yet. My client, Mr Derwent, only died at the beginning of last week.'

Meade had looked up sharply at the mention of Derwent's name, and Railton remembered that the events of Colombury had been reported in the national press. However, the manager made no immediate comment, but read rapidly through the will. When he had finished, he said casually, 'I take it this is the Peter Derwent who was found shot in some woods in the Cotswolds last week?'

'Yes,' said Railton. 'I'm his executor and in that capacity it's important for me to get in touch with an Arthur William Derwent. That's where I hope you can help me, Mr Meade. It seems he's had an account here at this branch of your bank for some years.'

'Is that so?' Meade raised his eyebrows. 'Arthur William Derwent? He's mentioned in the will, I suppose?'

'No.' Railton paused, choosing his words carefully. 'It's like this. We've got reason to suppose that Arthur Derwent may be indigent, or at least almost totally dependent upon a monthly allowance from the deceased. Mrs Derwent — the widow — wishes to ascertain if this is so, because something must be done for Arthur if it's necessary. The estate isn't large — far from it — and there are children. Between you and me —' Railton leant forward confidentially — 'Mrs Derwent could do with the money. Nevertheless if Arthur Derwent's in real need . . .'

'I understand. Very commendable of Mrs Derwent, if I may say so.' The bank manager gave a little bow in acknowledgement of the widow's attitude. 'But how can I help you?'

'We've got no address for Arthur Derwent, nor any contact with him. But the money — two hundred pounds a month — was paid by Standing Order into his account with your bank. Mr Meade, I was hoping that — in the strictest confidence, of course — you might be able to tell me something of his circumstances, and perhaps help me to get in touch with him. I know that you'd automatically forward a letter, but you must admit that the situation is a little unusual, and — '

Meade didn't reply at once. He made a pyramid of his hands, and regarded it thoughtfully. Tim Railton braced himself for a firm refusal. Then Meade stood up.

'Mr Railton, I've got an uneasy feeling that it's the police who should be making these enquiries. But give me a few minutes and I'll see what we can do. Excuse me.'

He left his office and Railton waited, sipping at his cold coffee. He was helping himself to another biscuit when the bank manager returned, accompanied by a younger man whom he introduced as his deputy, Walter Brown.

Brown, it emerged, had actually met Arthur Derwent on only two occasions, when the account was opened and last Thursday, when it was closed. Railton stifled his surprise and let the deputy manager continue. Brown described Arthur Derwent as a shabby, rather down-at-heel individual, quiet and reticent, but with old-fashioned manners.

'I took a certain amount of interest in him,' Brown admitted. 'He wasn't exactly the sort of customer we're used to in this branch, and it was an unusual account. He opened it with a deposit of twenty-five pounds, which remained untouched. Then each month, a few days after the first, he would come in and draw out in cash the whole of the two hundred pounds that had been credited. There were no other transactions — none at all.'

'And last Thursday he closed the account,' Railton said. 'Did he give any explanation?'

'Only that his benefactor had died, and there'd be no further payments. I — I felt quite sorry for the poor man.' Brown threw his boss an apologetic glance. 'I know it was none of my business, but I asked him if this would make a great difference to his financial position, and he said it would. It seems he was just over sixty, though he looked older, and he didn't qualify for an old age pension. All he had was a pittance from the Church. He'd retired early because of ill health, and—'

'What?' Tim Railton swallowed hard. This time he was unable to suppress his surprise. 'I wasn't aware that Mr Arthur Derwent was a parson,' he said quickly to cover his confusion.

'Oh yes,' Brown said. 'He always wore his clerical collar, even though he'd retired. He appeared a very respectable person, you know—well-spoken and all that—though obviously not well off. I hope I didn't give you any other impression. We were glad to have him as a client,' he added, glancing at Meade.

'No, no, not at all,' said Railton hastily. 'I'm most grateful to you for your help. But you've convinced me I must seek out Mr Derwent as soon as possible and see what can be done for him. Now, can you help me there? An address, perhaps?'

Brown hesitated and looked hopefully at his boss. Meade said, 'Normally, as you pointed out, I'd say you should write to him here, but my deputy and I agree that perhaps the circumstances are exceptional. Mr Derwent didn't strike Brown as someone who would be prepared to ask for charity from any of the usual agencies, and it's always possible he might do something foolish. None of us would want that. So—'

Tim Railton's next move was obvious—to check out the address he had been given. Fortunately it was in the Paddington area, and therefore on his way out of London. Convenient for himself, he thought, and equally convenient for anyone else—any blackmailer—living in the Colombury area. Though this was a pretty weak argument in the absence of any other indications . . .

In fact, he had a good deal of difficulty in finding the address at all, and had almost decided it was non-existent when a helpful postman directed him. In a mean street, not far from Paddington Station, he found what he was looking for. It was a small newsagent's that also sold sweets and tobacco and a miscellany of other oddments. Framed boards beside the doorway displayed a multitude of postcard-sized advertisements for goods and services — many of them dubious — for sale or hire.

Railton went in. It took several minutes of argument and a five pound note left casually on the counter before he could elicit any information whatsoever. The owner of the shop finally agreed that he remembered the Reverend Arthur Derwent; he didn't number many clergymen among his customers. Derwent had used the shop as an accommodation address, paying a small fee six months in advance, and calling in very occasionally to collect his correspondence. 'You'd be surprised,' the shopkeeper said, suddenly waxing eloquent. 'We fill a real need — a social service, I call it. Lots of people need an address like this — well-dressed executive types and all. Letters they don't want sent home, you know — ' But Derwent had received very few letters, perhaps one or two a year, and had given no forwarding address.

That was all, but Railton was satisfied. The bank had required an address of some kind, and a fictitious one might have been dangerous; letters returned as undeliverable could conceivably have led to suspicion and enquiries. Whoever the blackmailer was, Railton thought, he was a very careful individual.

It was mid-afternoon by the time Tim Railton drove through Colombury to his office. There had been a lot of traffic and the journey had been tedious. He was feeling tired and hot. All he really wanted was to get home to a cool bath, but he knew that work would have piled up in his absence. As he expected, Mrs Kirby was waiting for him.

'Come along,' he said as he strode through the outer office and threw his briefcase on to his desk. 'Break it to me gently. What haven't I done?'

Mrs Kirby's expression reproached him for his facetiousness. She said, 'There's been another tragedy at Broadfields. Mrs Wilson—that's Mr Trevor Grayson's housekeeper—she rang first. She said Mr Grayson had been found shot in the woods—just like Mr Derwent.'

Railton sat down slowly and drew a deep breath. 'Trevor Grayson,' he repeated.

'Yes, Mr Railton. It's dreadful, isn't it? Another murder, it looks like. Mrs Derwent wants you to call her as soon as you get back.'

Railton nodded. It wasn't like the shock Peter Derwent's death had been. Peter was—had been—a life-long friend, Grayson a mere acquaintance. But it was a blow—a second killing that must inevitably be connected with the first.

'Okay. Get me Mrs Derwent,' he was saying, when the phone on his desk rang. Mrs Kirby picked up the receiver, said, 'One moment, please,' then to Railton. 'It's Superintendent Thorne for you, sir.'

Railton took the phone. He listened, replied, 'Yes I just got back. My secretary's just told me. No, Super-intendent. Mrs Wilson's got it a little wrong. It's true Grayson did consult me once or twice; at one time he thought he might be charged with dangerous driving after he'd killed a dog. But I wouldn't claim to be his solicitor. I think a London firm acted for him when he bought his house. And I've no knowledge of his will. I'm sorry . . . Yes, indeed.'

Tim Railton put down the receiver thoughtfully. He turned to his secretary and said, 'Mrs Kirby, everything else will have to wait. Get Mrs Derwent on the phone and say I'm on my way up to see her.'

CHAPTER 14

Lorna had spent most of the day trying not to think, doing what had to be done quite automatically—cleaning, coping with the laundry, answering the demands of the family, bandaging the hand that Nina had burnt while making yet more jam. But always, at the back of her mind, was constant, nagging worry.

When Tim Railton arrived she was alone in the kitchen, and she greeted him with utter relief. 'Trevor Grayson?' she said at once.

'I know. I know,' said Railton. 'I've already had Superintendent Thorne on the phone. I've got to see him later. That's why—'

'But do you think that Peter and Trevor—' interrupted Lorna.

'Were their deaths connected? That I don't know. But I've spent the day in London, and there's something I've got to talk to you about—before I see the police.'

'Talk to me?' Lorna said quickly. 'Tim has something else happened?'

'No, Lorna, not exactly,' Railton said hesitantly. 'It's—it's a matter concerned with Peter's estate. Look, it's a lovely evening. Can't you stop messing about in here and come for a walk in the garden. At least I'll get your full attention there.'

Lorna nodded her understanding, aware of Railton's tension. 'Okay, Tim. Just let me wash my hands.'

She glanced at Railton as they walked across the grass to a couple of chairs in the shade of a beech tree. 'You didn't tell me the truth just now, did you, Tim? Something else has happened.'

'In a way, yes. In London today I've learnt something rather surprising concerning Peter. Whether it's actually connected with Peter's death—or Grayson's for that matter—I don't know. On the face of it, it doesn't seem likely, but I'm a lawyer and an officer of the Court, and I simply can't withhold possibly relevant evidence from the police. Really, I should have told them already, but I thought you had a right to know first.'

'Well, what is it?' Lorna's voice was steady. 'What is it I should know first?'

'My dear.' He reached across and took her hand. 'There doesn't seem to be any doubt that Peter was being blackmailed. Each month . . .'

Lorna listened without interruption. She shook her head, but in amazement rather than disbelief. When Railton stopped speaking, she said slowly, 'It fits. The sale of Broadfields and the beginning of the payments. But why? For God's sake, why? What could Peter have done? What did he have to hide? In his position—with the sort of life we led here—what temptations were there—'

Railton got to his feet. 'I know, Lorna. It's hard to imagine. But you do understand I must phone Thorne, make an appointment to see him tomorrow at the latest. I'm afraid it'll probably mean more enquiries. Things may come to light—things that you and the family would much rather—'

'What do you mean? What things?'

'I've no idea, but—'

'No, of course not. I'm sorry, Tim. That's just what we've been saying. It's impossible to think what could be worse for Peter than losing Broadfields.' Lorna sighed with frustration. 'Tim, do you think Trevor Grayson was being blackmailed too?' And when he shrugged: 'But it doesn't make sense, if it's connected with their deaths. It's the wrong way round. Why should a successful blackmailer . . .' Then she added. 'What's more, clergyman or not, I refuse to believe Simon Kent had anything to do with it.'

'So do I, Lorna. Anyone can put on a dog-collar. But two similar murders in much the same place does suggest someone living in the neighbourhood. Anyway, it's no good trying to do the police's job for them. But you see I've got to tell them about Peter, don't you?'

'Yes. Yes, of course,' Lorna said, and added sadly almost to herself, 'When Peter was killed like that I thought things couldn't get any worse, any more frightening. But now they have — and there seems to be no end to it.'

Railton could think of no reply. He raised his arms in a helpless gesture, and turned and hurried across to the office in the stables where he could use the phone in privacy. He was angry at his inability to offer Lorna the comfort he would have liked to give her. And his anger made him more peremptory with the police than he might otherwise have been.

When Superintendent Thorne came on the line from Kidlington, he said, 'Superintendent, I'd be glad if you could come to my office tomorrow morning, preferably first thing.'

Thorne, who had just had a trying interview with his Chief Constable, took his time in answering. 'Important, is it, Mr Railton?' he said. 'You've remembered something since we spoke earlier?'

'In London today I acquired some information relating to Peter Derwent's estate, Superintendent. I've now consulted Mrs Derwent, and she's asked me to pass it on to you.'

'She has, has she?' said the Superintendent. 'If it's got anything to do with the murder —' He stopped, then continued, 'It's not urgent, you say. Tomorrow will do.'

'Yes. You're in Kidlington now, and it's not worth

bringing you back here to Colombury. I prefer not to discuss it on the phone.'

'Very well, Mr Railton. I'll be at your office at eight-thirty in the morning. Good evening to you.'

Before Railton could reply, Thorne broke the connection. Railton grinned wryly; he wasn't in the habit of getting to his office so early, but he had been a little abrupt and he could understand the Superintendent's feelings. Then his grin vanished. He was still holding the phone in his hand, and he'd distinctly heard a loud click on the line, as if the receiver had been replaced on an extension. Had someone been listening to his conversation with Thorne?

Richard came into the office at that moment, and saw his expression. 'Something wrong?'

'An odd noise on the phone, that's all. I can't believe the police are tapping it. And if they were, they'd be more efficient.'

'Oh Lord!' Richard laughed. 'It was probably Holly. At one time she was always listening in from the house. I hope it wasn't desperately private, Tim.'

'No. Very boring for her, in fact.'

'She's a problem at the moment, is Holly.' Richard was suddenly serious. 'We're all pretty fraught, though we're doing our best not to show it, but Holly's really been knocked for six. Her behaviour's quite unpredictable.'

'I'm not surprised,' Railton said.

'No,' said Richard. 'But the funny thing is she seems almost more upset by Trevor Grayson's death than by Dad's.' He broke off as Nina came into the office to ask if Railton would stay for supper. 'At least Aunt Nina's bearing up,' he went on when Nina had left. 'She's a wonderful old girl, isn't she?'

'It's not that she doesn't feel,' said Railton. 'She's got a will of iron. She's had a lot of sorrow in her life and learnt to bear it with fortitude.' Then, thinking this sounded unduly pompous, he changed the subject and enquired about Richard's grant. For the next few minutes, their current problems forgotten, they amicably discussed the legal profession and what it might have to offer.

After supper, a long and leisurely affair, the family continued to sit around the table, chatting and listening to John Derwent talk about the States. He was an engaging speaker and, Railton suspected, a good lecturer and teacher, able to make the dry dust of the law seem fascinating. Certainly he had the attention of his present audience — except for Holly, who was apparently completely absorbed in biting off the end of her thumb.

They were interrupted by the arrival of Dr Band, and at once Nina said, 'Is this a social call, Dick, or have you come to see me? Because if it's me, you can go away again. I've recovered from that bug and I don't need your ministrations.'

'I'm glad to hear it, Nina.' Band grinned. He was used to dealing with Nina Langden. 'What have you done to your hand?'

'Burnt it. It's nothing.' She turned on Lorna. 'You didn't —'

'No, I didn't,' Lorna said firmly. 'But it's a nasty burn, and since Dick's here he might as well have a look at it.'

'Of course I will.' Band didn't give Nina the chance to refuse. 'But really this call is neither social nor professional. I've come to you for help.'

'Help?' Lorna said.

They all stared at him, and the doctor looked slightly embarrassed. 'Not for myself,' he said at once. 'It's for Simon Kent.'

Railton, who had been intending to leave and was getting to his feet, sat down again. 'Tell us, Dick.'

Dr Band had been returning from a call in a nearby village. Driving past the rectory he had noticed that the front door was wide open, and some of the upstairs lights on, though it was still bright daylight. Without hesitation—as he said, a lot of strange things had been happening in the neighbourhood of Colombury recently—the doctor had stopped his car and gone to investigate.

'I walked straight into the hall,' he said, 'and called out. No one answered, so I looked around and finally went upstairs. Simon was lying on the floor of his bedroom, and—'

'Not another!' whispered Lorna, white-faced.

But Holly had jumped to her feet, knocking over the chair behind her. 'She's killed him! Mrs Kent's killed him!' she cried. She was wildly excited, her eyes very bright, colour flaming in her cheeks.

Nina acted swiftly. She pulled Holly down on to her lap. 'No, darling, no. Don't take on so.' She rocked the girl in her arms, at first fiercely then, as Holly offered no resistance, more gently.

Railton said, 'Simon? He's not really—'

'No, of course not,' Band said irritably. 'He's not dead. He's not even hurt. He's just drunk, but for God's sake let's keep that to ourselves—'

Nina stood up, still holding Holly close. 'I'm going to put this child to bed,' she said. 'She's completely overwrought, and it's not surprising. Come up in a few minutes, Dick, and have a look at her.'

'I'll be up to see you both.' Band smiled at Holly, who ignored him, her face buried in Nina's breast.

Lorna shook her head hopelessly as Nina led Holly from the room. 'I knew Holly didn't like Jean Kent,' she said, 'but I never realized she hated her.'

'Why should she?' John Derwent asked.

Clare answered for her mother. 'Mrs Kent's always chasing her away from the churchyard, and—and—I know it's absurd and I'm not sure I'm right, but from something Holly said, I think she's got hold of the idea that Mrs Kent killed Dad.'

'But that's crazy!'

'Why on earth—'

They all spoke at once, but Railton cut across the babble. Authoritatively he said, 'Let's leave it for now. Let's stop gossiping about Mrs Kent.' He turned to Dr Band. 'What can we do for Simon?'

The doctor began to explain. Apparently for some reason Simon Kent had drunk a considerable amount, been violently sick and passed out. 'To put it bluntly,' said Band, 'he's as tight as a coot. I cleaned him up a bit and put him to bed. The point is really that someone should be within call tonight. I doubt if he's used to monumental hangovers, and he might get up and have a fall. Or he could vomit again and choke, though I should think that's most unlikely. Anyway, he probably shouldn't be left alone and, seeing he's the Rector, I thought better of calling the district nurse or—'

'Of course you were right to come here, Dick,' Lorna said. 'I—I take it Jean wasn't there.'

'No. Nor her car.' He paused, and then added. 'And between ourselves, nor her clothes. I looked in her room. She's taken everything. I'm afraid it seems to me very much as if she's gone for good. Probably that's what made Simon take to the bottle.'

'I imagine she's gone to London,' said Lorna. 'She often does.'

'Look,' said Richard. 'I'll go over to the rectory and spend the night there. I'm a light sleeper, and I'll cope with the old boy if he needs any help.'

'That would be marvellous, Richard,' Band said. 'Don't hesitate to call me if you want to. I'll look in in the morning anyway.'

Railton seized his chance. 'It's time I was going myself,' he said. 'Get whatever you want for the night, Richard, and I'll give you a lift.'

So, while Lorna took the doctor up to see Holly and look at Nina's hand, Tim Railton drove Richard round to the rectory. Railton had merely intended to drop him there, but when they arrived curiosity and concern for the Rector combined to make him go into the house with Richard.

Band had locked up when he left, but had taken the backdoor key. Voices lowered, feeling a little like trespassers, the two men climbed the stairs. They found Simon Kent lying on his back, snoring gently. He was obviously in no danger, though he looked drawn and haggard, and his austerely furnished room smelt strongly of whisky and vomit in spite of the open window.

While Richard was deciding where to sleep, Railton wandered into the adjoining bedroom, which had clearly been Jean Kent's. As the doctor had said, however, most of the signs of her occupancy had been removed. The dressing-table was bare, and the sliding doors of the fitted cupboards that lined one wall were sufficiently open to show they were almost empty.

'Poor Simon,' Railton said under his breath. 'Pity she didn't leave him years ago.'

He glanced into one of the open cupboards, and his eye was caught by a glint of white. Some garment had been pushed back into a corner, perhaps forgotten. Idly Railton reached in, and brought out a grey trouser suit. Under it on the hanger were a white clerical collar and a black clerical vest. The suit was far from new—it could have been abandoned intentionally—and was obviously a woman's outfit because the jacket buttoned from right to left. But who would notice that, Railton thought, unless they were already suspicious? Brown, the assistant bank manager in London? Improbable. The Paddington shopkeeper? Just possibly, but to him, used to all sorts and conditions of people, it might not have seemed odd.

Railton thrust the suit back into the cupboard as Richard called to him. Jean Kent! A masculine type of woman, certainly, and often in London. Was it conceivable that she'd played the part of the Reverend Arthur William Derwent?

Tim Railton went back to the other bedroom slowly. It was just one more thing, he thought with regret, that he'd have to tell the Superintendent in the morning.

CHAPTER 15

The following morning Mrs Wilson showed Superintendent Thorne into Trevor Grayson's study. It was a small room, and a desk under the window took up almost the whole of one wall. A swivelling office chair stood before the desk, and the rest of the furniture consisted of a bookcase with a selection of routine reference works and a few paperbacks and magazines, a leather armchair and a side table with an electric typewriter.

'Mr Grayson didn't use it much,' the housekeeper said, seeing the direction of the Superintendent's glance. 'Just to write a few business letters, I think.'

Thorne nodded. 'Is there a safe anywhere?'

'No, sir. Mr Grayson said any half-competent burglar could crack a home safe. He preferred to keep his valuable papers at his London bank.'

But Mrs Wilson had no idea of the name or address of the bank. Sighing heavily, Thorne dismissed her and sat down at the desk. There was nothing for it but another long morning looking through files and documents. But for a full minute the Superintendent did nothing, his mind reflecting on what Railton had told him during their meeting at eight-thirty. Briefly and bluntly, it seemed that Peter Derwent had over the years been subject to blackmail by a Reverend Arthur William Derwent, who might in reality have been Mrs Jean Kent. It was an interesting story, if true, but it need have no necessary connection with the killings — especially if Peter Derwent had been killed in mistake for Trevor Grayson because he was wearing Grayson's distinctive oilskin.

Anyway, thought the Superintendent, the main thing was to keep a clear head, and concentrate for the moment on Grayson. Who benefited from his death? Who might have wanted him dead? Maybe the contents of the desk would help. Thorne got down to work. With one exception, the desk drawers were all unlocked, and he went through their contents carefully. Grayson had kept a local account, presumably for convenience, but his main bank seemed to be in Oxford.

Thorne frowned. No clue yet to a London bank. A slim address book that would have to be gone through in detail, but no obvious mention of a solicitor. Choosing the obvious key from the bunch found in Grayson's pocket, Thorne unlocked the remaining desk drawer.

This was it. This was what he'd been looking for. A file of correspondence with a Trust Company in London. Evidently it had looked after all Grayson's financial affairs. The Company — or its solicitors — had negotiated the purchase of the cottage, drawn up his will, and were named as his executors. What was more, Thorne was delighted to find, a copy of the will was included in the file.

It was of very considerable interest. Grayson had left a thousand pounds, tax paid, to his housekeeper, Mrs Wilson, for every year she remained in his employment. His cottage and its entire contents — again tax free — went to Richard, son of Peter Derwent of Broadfields. The residue of the estate was bequeathed to the Reverend Simon Kent, on condition that he spent a reasonable sum on a suitable plaque to be erected in a wall of St Mary's Church in memory of Michael Derwent.

At least it was clear who would profit from Grayson's murder, Thorne thought, though whether this would help was another matter. Mrs Wilson he could almost certainly dismiss. She would acquire a few thousand pounds, but she had lost a good job that might be hard to replace. Richard Derwent, however, stood to gain a nice little property and, depending on the size of the estate, the Rector could do well. So far he hadn't considered either Richard Derwent or Kent as serious suspects; now he might have to think again. And always, looming in the background, was Peter Derwent's own death, which mustn't be ignored.

Thorne gently stroked his moustache as he considered the position. Anyway, there was no doubt about his next move. He was replacing the receiver after the second of a couple of phone calls to London when he was interrupted by a tap at the door. Mrs Wilson announced Sergeant Abbot, and asked if they would like coffee.

'Please,' Thorne said, and when she'd gone, 'Well, Abbot, any luck?'

'Not with the gun, sir. They've not found it.'

'I'll swear the bloody thing's there somewhere. All our suspects have been going in and out of those damned woods as if they were a set of revolving doors, and not one of them's been carrying anything like a .22 rifle.'

'Yes, sir,' said Sergeant Abbot dutifully. 'But if it's there, it's very well hidden. The woods aren't easy to search, but the whole area's been gone over very carefully. The boys have been doing a thorough job, sir,' he added.

'I'm glad to hear it,' said Thorne wearily, then immediately looked more cheerful as Mrs Wilson appeared with a coffee tray. 'Anything else, Abbot?'

'Yes. All of it negative. Joe Wilson's in the clear as far

as Grayson's death's concerned. He was serving behind the bar in his pub from twelve till three on Tuesday, and the girl who helps him swears he was around a good hour before and after—getting ready for opening and clearing up and so on.' Abbot suddenly grinned. 'Incidentally, sir. I'm told he's put that motor-bike of his up for sale. You've certainly scared him off that girlfriend.'

Thorne nodded, but made no comment. 'And?' he said.

'Nothing much, really. Mr Railton would seem to have been at his office at the relevant times, leastways, his car didn't leave the courtyard all day, and he had sandwiches sent in instead of going over to the Windrush Arms for lunch. Tom Meakin was seen at the far end of his farm around noon and, for what it's worth, Sergeant Court says he's got a big mouth but he wouldn't hurt a fly. And the Reverend Simon Kent was in Colombury visiting the butcher's wife; their daughter's getting married at St Mary's in a couple of weeks.' Abbot drew breath. 'That's all, sir.'

'Enough to be going on with,' Thorne said. 'Now I'll bring you up to date.' Five minutes later he concluded, 'I've just been on to his Trust Company, and they confirm this is the will they hold. They also say Grayson had a box in their safe deposit, and I've made arrangements with them and the Met for us to see it opened this afternoon. But the first thing right now is to get along to the rectory.'

Richard greeted the two police officers at the front door of the rectory. 'Mr Kent's not available,' he said abruptly. 'He's—unwell. And Mrs Kent's not here. She's gone to London.'

'Yes, yes. We know all about that. But we've got to see Mr Kent, nevertheless.'

Thorne spoke coldly. He had no intention of being thwarted by Richard Derwent, who somewhat unwillingly showed the detectives into the sitting-room. Here they found Simon Kent, still in his dressing-gown, looking wan and ill, and Nina Langden urging him to drink a large mug of black coffee she had just made.

Kent raised his head from his hands and stared at Thorne and Abbot without warmth. 'Not more questions,' he said. 'Jean told me about them. I dare say she'd have left me sooner or later in any case, but I really think it was your questions that were the last straw—' He shook his head, and groaned as pain shot through his temples.

Nina protested. 'Superintendent, you can see how he is. Surely your business can wait till tomorrow. Give the poor man a chance to recover.'

'No.' Thorne was quite uncompromising. 'Some points are urgent.' Without being asked, he pulled up a chair and sat down opposite the Rector. 'Mr Kent, I'm sorry to hear of your wife's sudden departure, but it's about her I must ask you. You told me she'd received an inheritance from an aunt some years ago. Are you sure of that?'

Kent looked puzzled. 'Sure of it? Of course I'm sure. She got a lump sum and a monthly allowance for the rest of her life. After that the capital went to her nieces. The solicitor explained it to both of us very carefully.'

'You met the solicitor?'

'Yes. He came to see us. He had a son up at Oxford, I remember, so it was quite convenient.'

'Do you recall his name?'

'Yes, I do.' Simon Kent, momentarily distracted from his hangover, smiled triumphantly. 'It was such a strange name—Kettledrum.'

'Kettledrum!' Richard broke in. 'But I know the son—Philip Kettledrum. He was up at my college. His father was the senior partner of one of those highly respected London family firms. In Maiden Lane, I think.'

'Many thanks.' The Superintendent produced a

spuriously benevolent smile. 'Now, Mr Kent, I imagine
you know your wife's present address. Or did she just—'

'No, no, no. It wasn't like that. We parted quite
amicably,' said Kent wearily. 'It had been coming on for a
long time. She's gone to stay with a woman friend of hers
in London indefinitely. I've got the address here. It's off
Knightsbridge. I told you she went up to London once a
month or so.'

'Yes,' said Thorne.

'But what's this about? Why are you interested in Jean?
She can't have anything to do with your enquiries. Why
on earth should she have wanted to harm Peter Derwent
or Grayson?'

Thorne wasn't prepared to admit that he had no idea.
Her absence of motive was one of the things that had been
bothering him. Of all the possible suspects she alone
seemed to have none. Instead he said, 'Your wife, I
gather, was a good shot. At least she used to shoot rooks,
and that's not easy. Could I see Mrs Kent's rifle?'

'She didn't own one.'

'What?'

'She borrowed a sporting rifle from us now and then,'
Nina Langden said. 'But we haven't got the one she
generally used. I'm sure we told you, Superintendent.
One was stolen before Christmas.'

'I remember,' Thorne said. He paused and looked
around the room as if considering his next question. Then
he said, 'Mr Kent, your wife was rather fond of wearing
trouser suits.'

Kent stared at him. 'Yes,' he said, 'That's true.
Personally, I wasn't sure they were right for all occasions.
But what—'

'It's all right, Mr Kent,' Thorne said soothingly. 'It's
just that we know Mrs Kent possessed a grey trouser
suit—clerical grey, you might call it.'

The Rector's reaction was unexpected. His face had

been pale, but now he flushed, blushed almost. He looked rather hopelessly at Richard and Nina.

Thorne plunged straight on. 'Yesterday Mrs Kent's grey suit was hanging in her wardrobe, with a clerical collar and vest hanging under it. Did you know your wife was in the habit of dressing up as a clergyman, Mr Kent?'

Simon Kent had recovered himself. He struggled to his feet to confront the Superintendent. 'Yes, Superintendent, of course I knew, though I can't see what business it is of yours. She wanted to wear a clerical collar at a church fancy dress party some years ago, but I forbade it. So she'd wear it in the house occasionally—to rile me, I think. But not for years. Not since—'

'Not since? Go on, Mr Kent.'

'I hit her,' Kent said. 'I smacked her face. The doorbell rang and she answered it—in that costume! The door of the rectory! It was almost sacrilege! I told her if she ever did such a thing again I'd turn her out of the house, and she believed me. It was before her aunt died, and she was still dependent on me. But I hit her. I'm still ashamed when I think of it. But it could have been anyone on the doorstep. Thank God it was Trevor Grayson.'

'Grayson?' Thorne tried hard to swallow his surprise, but the exclamation had already escaped.

'Yes. He'd come to ask about Michael's grave. It was his first visit to Colombury—before he came to live here—and for a moment he mistook Jean for me. It was horribly embarrassing, but he never mentioned the incident again, to me or anyone else, as far as I know. Poor Trevor. He was a good, kind man.'

Thorne had one more point to make. Now was the chance. 'He liked you too, Mr Kent,' he said. 'It looks as if Mr Grayson remembered you in his will.'

'He did? Me—or the church?' The pale face lit up. 'It doesn't matter. How kind of him!'

There was no doubting the Rector's sincerity, Thorne

thought. Whatever his wife might or might not have done, Simon Kent had played no part in it.

'And you, Mr Derwent.' Thorne turned to Richard. 'I believe you're also to be a beneficiary.'

'Under Grayson's will? Don't be silly. Why should Grayson leave me anything?' Richard laughed, and Thorne could have sworn he was as surprised as Kent had been. 'Lucky I was in Oxford when he was killed so I've got an alibi. How much?'

'Richard!' Nina Langden was shocked.

'Why not? I might as well be practical. I can certainly do with some cash.'

'But not from Trevor Grayson. It's—it's—' Visibly upset, Nina seemed unable to find adequate words. 'Why should he leave you anything at all?'

Richard shrugged, and it was Thorne who answered. 'Perhaps in memory of Michael Derwent,' he said quietly. If he was hoping for any reaction, he was disappointed. He received only blank stares.

Immediately after an early lunch Superintendent Thorne and Sergeant Abbot drove up to London. They made a brief call at Scotland Yard, and then presented themselves at the offices of Kettledrum, Kettledrum and Fyfe—indeed a name to remember—in Maiden Lane. Here Mr Kettledrum Senior confirmed what Simon Kent had said. Jean Kent was in receipt of a small monthly income from the estate of her late aunt. 'There's no secret about it,' the lawyer said. 'The will was probated years ago.'

'She might have wanted—or needed—more,' Abbot commented as they left the lawyer's office.

'She might,' Thorne agreed noncommittally.

They next called on Mr Brown, the deputy manager of the bank to which Arthur William Derwent's payments had been made, and pressed him for a more precise description of his customer. The picture he drew was that of a heavy well-muscled character—someone who couldn't possibly have been a woman. And Jean Kent, when they interviewed her in her friend's luxurious house near Knightsbridge, was surprisingly forthcoming.

In fact, when asked about her clerical garb, she merely laughed. 'Of course I teased him about his ridiculous dog-collar,' she said, 'especially after the fuss he made about that stupid party. Anyway, modern clergymen don't bother with dog-collars and things like that. And when he hit me! I'd have left him there and then, but I'd no money. Even when my aunt died there wasn't really enough, and I hadn't yet met my friend. But she's been suggesting for some time that I should come and live with her, and now I'm sure our friendship is a lasting one, I've come. What else do you want to know about my private life, Superintendent?'

'Your relationship with Trevor Grayson?' suggested Thorne.

'Practically non-existent. Superintendent, I didn't kill Grayson—or Peter Derwent either. You shouldn't believe all the lies you're told.' She was suddenly vindictive. 'It's that little bitch Holly who's been getting at you, I'll be bound. She's wasting your time.'

The two officers took a taxi to the City. On the way Abbot asked, a little anxiously, 'Do you think she's right, sir? That we've been wasting our time?'

'Some of it, I'm sure,' said Thorne cheerfully. 'But we're learning. We're learning.'

What they were learning that was relevant to the case, Abbot wasn't sure. But he had little time to ruminate, for at the Trust Company they found that preparations had been made for their reception. Their credentials were checked and they were then given access to the files relating to Grayson's affairs. These did little more than confirm what Thorne had already gathered on the phone; the last will and testament of which he had a copy was identical with the original held by the Trust.

Finally in the presence of two executives of the company, Thorne was allowed to use a key he had found on Grayson's bunch to help open the safe-deposit box in the vault. Here, in the usual small, windowless room, they all inspected and itemized the contents. Most of these were routine: the deeds of Grayson's house in Colombury, another copy of his will, insurance policies, some bonds and a list of his investments. The latter corresponded exactly with the holdings administered on his behalf by the Trust Company. Grayson, though not wealthy, had been very comfortably off.

There was only one item that gripped Superintendent Thorne's interest. This was a copy of a death certificate dated nearly four years ago. A man had died of a cerebral hæmorrhage in what appeared to be a mental hospital in Reading. The age of the victim was forty-three, and his name was given as Arthur Williams.

CHAPTER 16

'Be a dear,' Lorna said. 'Run over to the rectory and ask Mr Kent if he'd like to have supper with us tonight.'

Holly stopped biting the end of her thumb. It was an ideal errand for what she had in mind. 'Okay, Mum,' she said cheerfully.

She took the request literally and set off at a run, but soon slowed to a more ruminative walk. She wondered if she dare go into the woods. Officially they were still out of bounds. She could see the white tape the police had strung between trees to take in an irregular area, and the occasional warning notice. But even at eleven o'clock in the morning there was no one about and no obvious sign of police activity.

She delivered her message at the rectory. Simon Kent, who had recovered from his hangover and was looking relatively normal again, said he'd be delighted to accept Lorna's invitation. He produced a couple of chocolate biscuits, and with one in each hand Holly wandered off to the churchyard. Now that Mrs Kent had gone, she could do what she liked without hindrance or recriminations. For a while she walked among the Derwent graves. Then she picked some daisies and scattered them over the mound of earth beneath which her father lay. Finally she went and sat on the churchyard wall.

From here she had a good view of the edge of the wood nearest to her. She remained very still for some while, watching, but still saw no one. When she slid over the wall she knew exactly which way she would go. This morning she had carefully put on khaki shorts and a green shirt, camouflage in case she had the chance to enter what she thought of as the danger zone.

Making herself as small and inconspicuous as possible, she dodged among the bushes until she reached the trees, where she turned and looked back. So far she had done nothing wrong, and now no one could see her, except perhaps the Rector if he happened to be at one of his upstairs windows.

The day was warm and overcast, and in the woods it was gloomy. Holly was surprised to find she felt nervous. She moved swiftly along the main path until she found the place she wanted. She had just turned off the path into the undergrowth when there was a sudden shout.

'Hi there! Where d'you think you're going?'

Holly jumped. She had been unaware of the man behind her. She swung round, her heart thumping, her eyes bright with fear. She had never seen him before, and had no means of knowing he was one of Thorne's team from Kidlington. For a moment, she thought he might be a journalist—there had been several about—but she didn't like him.

He was now between her and the path, and she hesitated to run further into the undergrowth, and perhaps lead him towards the tree where the rifle was hidden. Instead, she suddenly feinted to his right, then tried to dive past him on his left.

She was out of luck. The man was quick and left-handed. He seized her tightly by the arm. She opened her mouth to scream but he clamped a large hand over it. Holly bit him.

The man swore. 'You little devil!' But he didn't release her as she'd hoped. He did, however, remove his hand from her mouth, and at once she screamed and screamed with all the power of her lungs.

Footsteps came running, and Holly sighed with relief when she recognized Sergeant Court. The Sergeant took in the situation at a glance. 'It's all right, Miss Holly,' he said. 'No one's going to hurt you.'

'Hurt her! She hurt me, damn it. She bit me. Look at my hand. The little—' This time he used a four-letter word Holly had never heard before. 'She's dangerous, a bloody menace.'

To her surprise Holly found it quite easy to burst into tears. 'I'm sorry,' she said between sobs. 'I'm sorry. I didn't mean it. He frightened me.'

'What were you doing here anyway? You know you shouldn't be in the woods.' Court, who had a daughter of Holly's age, did his best to sound severe. 'You mustn't come here again till you're told you can. You understand?'

Holly nodded. 'I was just—just playing,' she said. 'Pretending to be a—a police detective. Can I go home now?'

'I'll take you,' Court said. 'And have a word with your mother.'

The other man, who was wrapping a handkerchief around his injured hand, snorted. 'Tell her mother if I catch her in the woods again I'll tan the hide off her.'

'Okay,' Court said. 'Come along, Miss Holly.'

Holly, trying to look as abject as possible, followed Sergeant Court along the path. He walked fast, and she had to trot to keep up with him. In fact, her brain was working as quickly as her legs. There were some questions she wanted to ask, but she couldn't risk arousing his suspicions.

'Sergeant, when shall I be able to go into the woods again?' she commenced breathlessly.

Court slowed his pace. 'When Superintendent Thorne decides.'

It was an unsatisfactory answer. 'But what are you doing here all this time?'

'Looking for the weapon that killed Mr Grayson.' Court saw no point in not being blunt.

It was what Holly had feared, but at least it showed they hadn't found the rifle yet. On the other hand, how was she going to retrieve it, with the woods full of policemen? She daren't be caught in that particular spot again.

Then the Sergent volunteered, 'If we don't have any luck in the next day or two I think the Super'll give up. We can't get a line on the weapon ourselves, and the villain hasn't come back to get it as we hoped he might. So there's not much else we can do. I guess the woods'll be open again before too long. But till they are . . .'

Holly gave him her solemn word that she would pay attention to his warnings. She took less kindly to her mother's reproofs when Court handed her over. Lorna was angry, and didn't spare her.

'Why do you have to be so stupid, Holly? I send you to the rectory with a perfectly simple message, and instead you wander off where you know you're not supposed to go. Why?'

'I like the woods. And anyway I'd delivered your old message. Mr Kent's coming to supper.'

Lorna sighed with exasperation. 'For God's sake, Holly, don't be so difficult. Can't you try to help instead of hindering? If you want to be outside there's plenty to do in the stables.'

'No! Clare's sure to be there mooning about with John, though how she can think she loves him when he's taken Broadfields away from us I —'

'John is taking nothing that isn't legally his,' Lorna said firmly. 'Now stop this nonsense. If you don't want to go out to the stables, go and find Aunt Nina. She's having a lot of difficulty with that burnt hand of hers. It takes her twice as long to do the simplest things.'

'Okay.'

'And don't let me catch you anywhere near the woods until I give you permission myself — never mind the police. It could be dangerous, Holly. You might — you might even get shot.'

Holly glowered, and muttered something that sounded like, 'Not me, silly.' But she was already running from the room, and Lorna didn't call her back to ask her to explain. There was work to be done and Lorna started to vacuum the sitting-room carpet, her thoughts not on Holly, but on her older daughter and John Derwent.

In fact, Clare and John were not together in the stables. John Derwent had driven into Colombury and was at that moment in the offices of Railton, Mercer and Grey, sitting across the desk from Tim Railton. He was trying, as he said, to make his position clear.

'I've got to return to Boston in a few days, and I'd like to reach a decision about the future of Broadfields before I go. Richard and I have talked it over, but —'

'One minute, John.' Railton held up a restraining hand. 'In the first place, it's nothing to do with Richard. Apart from a few small gifts, Lorna is Peter Derwent's sole heir. And secondly, you don't obtain possession of Broadfields for a year.'

'I know all that. But let's get one thing straight to start with. I don't want Broadfields. I never have. If I'd been consulted at the time I'd have advised giving Cousin Peter the money he seemed to need, or at least making him an interest-free loan. But my father, though he was a hard-headed businessman, had a sentimental streak. He liked the idea that the old Derwent home might be occupied by me, or if not by me perhaps by a grandson of his. So, kidding himself he was being generous, he offered Cousin Peter this crazy agreement, and Peter seems to have been desperate enough to take it. Presumably the poor guy had no choice. An offer he couldn't refuse, and all that sort of thing.'

'I see.' Railton smiled wryly. 'I wondered just how it had come about.'

'Poor Pa,' John Derwent continued. 'There were two things he didn't really appreciate. The first is that it really doesn't matter who lives at Broadfields. Richard's the head of the Derwent family, whatever that means, and would remain so. That's why I talked it over with him. And, of course, Broadfields is far from being what it used to be. The size it is now, after so much land's been sold, I doubt if it's a viable proposition as a working estate.'

Tim Railton took off his spectacles and polished them. John Derwent seemed to know all the answers, and to have made up his own mind what to do.

Railton said, 'Do I take it then that you'll be selling Broadfields as soon as you have possession? Have you told Lorna?'

'Not yet, but that's the general idea. If Richard had wanted the place it might have been different but, as you know, he doesn't. He agrees with me about its long-term possibilities as a going concern. And I gather there isn't enough money for Lorna to keep it up even if I let them stay on rent-free indefinitely. I'm right, yes?'

Railton nodded.

John said, 'Now, Grayson's cottage. Did you know that, according to Superintendent Thorne who's seen the will, Grayson left his cottage to Richard?'

'To Richard?' Railton was astonished. 'No, I'd no idea.'

'How big is it?'

'Well it's a nice property—certainly much easier to sell than Broadfields will be. But too small for all four of them, if that's what you're thinking.'

'Not four of them.' John grinned, and the Derwent charm suddenly became striking. 'I've made up my mind. I want to marry Clare, and I intend to ask her before I leave for home. I think she knows that, and I guess I know what her answer'll be.'

'Congratulations!' Railton said. His mind was racing. Here was a solution to all their problems. Clare in the States, happily married to John. Nina at the cottage—she might not like the idea at first, but she'd soon get accustomed to it, especially when she found she'd got Richard and Holly to look after. Because Lorna—Lorna could at last marry him. He wondered if all this was really feasible. Surely, he thought bitterly, it was too good to be true.

The Reverend Simon Kent was also considering the future. Now that he had got over the initial shock of his wife's departure, he'd come to accept the fact that he would undoubtedly be much happier without her. He liked being a country priest, he loved the old church of St Mary and he had many friends in the neighbourhood. He wouldn't miss Jean. Nor, he thought ruefully, would the parish; she had never played her part there. With the money he hoped to receive from poor Trevor Grayson . . .

Lost in thought, Simon Kent prepared to leave the rectory for supper with the Derwents. He was on the point of shutting the front door behind him when he heard the phone begin to ring. He hesitated. It might be Jean, in which case he didn't want to answer. But it could be a sick parishioner, or . . . Reluctantly, he went back into the house.

In the event, the caller was Superintendent Thorne. 'Sorry to bother you again, Mr Kent, but I've a small problem, and perhaps you can help me.'

'Of course, if I can,' Kent said automatically.

'Cast your mind back to the afternoon you found Peter Derwent in the woods. You told us he murmured a name—the last thing he said before he died.'

'Yes. It was Wilson. I told you. I knew because I thought at once of—'

'Are you certain? Absolutely certain, Mr Kent? Please think carefully. You were bending over him, your face close to his. He can't have spoken above a whisper. Could it have been any other name. Williams, for example?'

'Will-iams?' Simon Kent tried out the word slowly. 'No. It's not possible. I remember quite clearly. Peter said, "Lorna". Then there was a pause. Then he said, "and the—children". Another pause. Finally he said, "Wil-son".'

There was an odd sound on the line. 'Just like that, Mr Kent? As if it were two syllables?'

'Yes. Everything was hesitant. He was having difficulty breathing or speaking at all. But I'm quite sure the name was Wilson, not Williams, Superintendent.'

'Wil-son. Will. Son. Is that how it was?'

'Exactly, Superintendent. I'm sorry if you hoped it might have been Williams.'

'On the contrary, Mr Kent. I'm most grateful to you. Many thanks, sir.'

Simon Kent nearly said, 'What for?' but the line had gone dead. And, now late, he hurriedly set off for Broadfields, wondering if anyone there might be able to identify the mysterious Williams.

CHAPTER 17

The weekend passed without further incident. A threatened thunderstorm did not materialize, but heavy rain soaked the team of men searching yet again for the murder weapon in the woods adjoining Broadfields. Every bush, every hole in the ground, every patch of undergrowth and hollow tree-trunk was probed and examined, but success eluded them. They found nothing.

Finally on Monday morning Superintendent Thorne admitted himself beaten, and ordered the police tapes and notices to be removed and the patrols to be abandoned. As a courtesy to the owners of the property he phoned Broadfields from Kidlington later in the day to inform them of the fact.

Lorna answered and, in turn, apologized for Holly's behaviour the previous Friday. Thorne, whom a kindly Sergeant Court had kept in ignorance of the matter, was furious. He immediately called the Sergeant and demanded a full report.

'And you call that playing?' he said when he had heard the full story. 'Biting a police officer?'

'He frightened her, sir. She was in tears.'

'Exactly where was all this?'

'Just off the main path, sir.' Court described the spot accurately.

Thorne grunted. 'If you catch that child doing anything else even vaguely odd, I want to know about it. Understood?'

Banging down the receiver before Court could answer, he made a small red mark on the large-scale map of the area that lay on his desk. For some seconds he stared at it, but it offered no immediate inspiration, so he returned to the files on the case.

There was a good deal of new material to be studied. The police hadn't been idle over the weekend. Apart from the renewed search of the woods, enquiries about Trevor Grayson had continued, and a visit had been paid to the mental hospital where Arthur Williams had apparently been a patient. It was this report which particularly interested the Superintendent. He regretted he hadn't made the expedition to Reading himself, but the demands of the Chief Constable and general pressure of work had forced him to delegate the job. He made a note to follow it up personally.

The mental hospital was, in fact, a private institution. Patients were voluntary and fee-paying, but the fees were kept to a minimum as the home was run as a charity by a religious order. Conditions were spartan but perfectly adequate.

The Reading detectives had been lucky. The chief medical officer and the matron had remained unchanged over the years, and both remembered Williams well, as did one of the nurses who had been in charge of the case. The circumstances of Williams's admission, eighteen months before he died, were a little unusual, but not unreasonably so. As far as the hospital knew, Williams had received a blow on the head in some sort of brawl in Africa somewhere, as a result of which he had suffered brain damage—not of a kind to threaten his life, but sufficient to make him a total amnesiac, subject to recurrent fits of mental regression. After local treatment had failed, he had been sent back to England and his friend, Trevor Grayson, had assumed responsibility for him. He had eventually been admitted to the Reading institution on the advice of a London specialist. He had been a docile and compliant patient, giving no trouble. The haemorrhage from which he had so tragically died in his sleep had been totally unexpected.

Grayson had said that Williams was without relatives, but he himself had visited the patient frequently. He had been responsible for all the fees, and for the eventual funeral expenses. Naturally, he had attended the funeral. The staff of the hospital, from the medical officer and the matron downwards, were full of praise for Mr Trevor Grayson's truly Christian behaviour.

Superintendent Thorne shook his head somewhat sceptically; he found this picture of Grayson as a kind, generous friend a little hard to take. All the indications were that Grayson had been blackmailing Derwent — the sequence of events when Grayson had arrived in Colombury, the death certificate in Grayson's safe-deposit box and the coincidence of names with its obvious inference that the friend of Arthur Williams had posed as the Reverend Arthur William Derwent. Yet Arthur Williams had been dead for years, and it was hard to imagine the reason for the blackmail, unless . . .'

Thinking of names, the Superintendent's mind switched to Peter Derwent's dying words. There was a world of difference between one word or two. Derwent had probably said Will-Son, not Wilson. He might have been contemplating his own will, and regretting he had nothing to leave his son, or even Grayson's will, if Grayson had told him he intended to leave the cottage to Richard. If Derwent's words could be explained in some such way, at least it cleared up one small mystery.

As he was fond of telling his junior officers, murders, in Thorne's experience, were rarely complex. They only seemed so during investigation because so much irrelevant or unimportant information had to be collected and collated. The problem was to sift the wheat from the

chaff, or in this particular case—he grinned to himself at
his simple joke—to see the wood through the trees. And
he thought he might be beginning to do just that, though
there were still plenty of diseased elms in the way.

The Superintendent was disturbed by a knock at his
office door. Sergeant Abbot was in the room almost at
once. 'Sir,' he said excitedly. 'Colombury's been on the
blower. Sergeant Court. There's been another shooting in
the Broadfields woods.'

Long before Superintendent Thorne had phoned, the
Derwents had known that the police had withdrawn from
the woods, and that they were no longer out of bounds.
Nina Langden, laboriously making her bed one-
handed—her burnt hand was still painful and
unusable—had glanced out of her window and seen the
officers removing their tapes and notices.

'At least we can go and explore those woods now,' John
Derwent said to Clare as he helped her prepare for a pony
class later in the morning. 'I'm curious to see them
properly, and you can show me where you played as a
kid.' He grinned at her. 'What about this afternoon? Or
do you have more pupils?'

'No. I've dressage with Betty Meakin from two to three,
but I'm free after that—apart from coping with the
horses,' Clare said. 'There's always such an awful lot to
do. I don't know how I'll manage when you've gone and
Richard's working.'

'That's something we might discuss this afternoon,'
John said casually. 'If I can have you to myself then,
unencumbered by family and animals.'

Clare laughed, colour rising in her cheeks. 'Okay. It's a
date, John. I've not been in the woods since—since Dad
was killed, but that's silly. I've got to get used to going
through them again.'

In the event the woods held no terrors for her. It was a

bright, sunny day, light poured down through the leaves and the place seemed warm and friendly. Clare relaxed in John Derwent's presence.

John talked, about Boston, his work at Harvard, his social life, his sister and her family. 'You'd like it over there, Clare,' he said.

'I'm sure I should,' she said.

'Great. Then come back with me. Marry me. My sister'll arrange everything. Or here, before we go. We could get a special licence. You don't want a huge white wedding, do you?'

'Of course not.'

'But you will marry me?'

Clare didn't hesitate. 'Yes,' she said. 'I've been waiting for you to ask me.'

She turned to him, smiling. Then suddenly there was a strange sound. A clink of metal against wood. A slithering noise, twigs breaking. A light thud. And a small muted cry that just possibly could have been a bird. They stared at each other, perfectly still.

'What the hell was that?' John whispered.

'I don't know.' Clare shivered. 'John, let's go.'

At once there was a louder noise, more slithering, a much heavier thud and this time an unmistakably human cry. John started forward, but Clare gripped his arm. 'No. Don't go. We'll get the police.'

'We must look. Someone could be badly hurt.' John released his arm from her grip. 'You go home and fetch Richard. I'll be okay.'

But Clare wasn't prepared to leave him. Amid the continual murmuring sounds of the woods she thought she heard someone moving. 'Over there!' she said, pointing, 'where the undergrowth's been flattened at the side of the path.'

John began to run, and Clare followed. She was so close behind that when he burst into a small clearing and stopped dead, she almost ran into his back. There was a moment of silence.

Then John said, very levelly, 'Hi, Holly!'

Holly Derwent stood with her back against a big tree. She was breathing hard, her flat child's chest rising and falling rapidly. There was a long scratch down one side of her face, her leg was grazed and her shirt torn. In her hands she held a .22 rifle, its barrel pointing at the ground.

Clare edged around John. 'Holly, how clever of you! You've found the rifle. I suppose it was up in the Nest. Of course the police wouldn't think of looking there.' She spoke quickly but calmly.

'What's the Nest?' John asked, not taking his eyes off Holly.

'It's the name we gave our old tree-house. It's not been used for years, but it was a wonderful place. Look! The tree it's in is quite unclimbable. You can only get to it by climbing that tree over there and then edging along a branch—'

While Clare was speaking, John had begun to move slowly towards Holly. He was not exactly sure what was happening, but he knew that the child's almost catatonic posture was unnatural, and that the last thing she should be holding was a weapon. He was half-expecting a violent reaction, and it came.

'Stop!' Holly screamed suddenly. 'Stop! I'll shoot if you come any closer.' She had lifted the rifle and was aiming it directly at John. Her eyes were wide, her long face pale beneath the tan, but her arms were perfectly steady. John Derwent had no doubt she meant what she said. He swallowed hard.

'Holly!' Clare was aghast. 'Holly, please!'

John knew he must try to wrest the initiative from the girl. 'Put that gun down at once!' His voice rang out authoritatively. 'At once!' he repeated. He measured the distance between them, and knew he couldn't make it.

'No!' cried Holly. As if mesmerized, she brought the barrel of the rifle up a careful inch, and slowly tightened her finger on the trigger.

Clare's movement was instantaneous. As Holly fired she flung herself at John, knocking him sideways so that he staggered, tripped and fell, hitting his head against the trunk of a tree. Temporarily he was stunned. It was Holly's chance. Taking the rifle with her, she ran.

Swearing, John Derwent tried to get to his feet, only to find that Clare was lying half on top of him. 'Are you okay, honey? Shift a bit so I can get up.' He moved, trying to ease her from him. Then he realized that his hand was hot and sticky with blood. 'Christ!' he whispered. 'Oh Christ!'

As quickly and carefully as he could he slid himself free and knelt beside Clare. She was unconscious, but breathing, and hope leapt in him. The next instant it was killed as he took in the widening stain of blood that spread across the front of her white shirt. What should he do? Scraps of half-digested information flitted across his mind. Don't move the patient. Staunch the bleeding. Make the victim as comfortable as possible. Keep the patient warm.

Tearing off his shirt, he ripped it in half. With one half he made a pad and laid it gently over where he believed the wound to be. The other half he used to tie around Clare's body to keep the pad tightly in place. Then he lifted her and began to carry her through the trees.

Clare had the narrow bones of all the Derwents, but she was quite tall and, unconscious, no easy burden. Fortunately John was physically strong and in good training. He could manage to carry her, but he feared that with every step he was harming her further. Yet he couldn't have left her, he told himself as he staggered along, he couldn't have left her to die alone in that goddamned wood like her father.

Sweat was pouring off him as at last the path cleared the trees, and he came out into the open. It had been further than he had expected and, in spite of brief rests, he was exhausted. The house was still some distance away, but he laid Clare tenderly on the ground, and started to run.

As he neared the house a figure came through the archway leading to the stables. Stumbling to a halt, John waved and shouted, 'Richard!' For a moment he thought Richard, not understanding, would merely return his wave. But Richard had clearly sensed the urgency of his appeal and he came running.

'John, what is it? God! You're covered in blood.'

'Clare's been shot. I—I don't know how bad it is, but she's still alive. Over there.' Gasping, John pointed to where Clare lay.

Richard didn't bother with questions. 'Okay. Go back to her. We'll be with you right away.' He turned and ran. And John, almost reluctant in case he was too late, went back to Clare. She was still unconscious, but the bleeding didn't seem so bad and her breathing, though shallow, was steady. He sat beside her and held her hand, willing Richard to hurry.

In fact, Lorna was there within minutes, with blankets and a businesslike first aid kit. Richard followed, carrying a light camp bed.

'The doctor?' John asked urgently.

'He'll be here directly. Nina's phoning him right now.' Lorna managed a crooked smile. 'He'll do everything that's possible, John. He's a good friend, as you know.' Her voice shook, but her hands were steady as she opened Clare's bloody shirt and exposed the wound.

For once Sergeant Abbot had managed to startle the Superintendent. Thorne sat up sharply in his office chair in Kidlington, pulled at his moustached upper lip and snapped, 'All right. Tell me! Who?'

'I don't know, sir.'

'You don't know who's been shot?' Thorne cast his eyes upwards towards the ceiling. 'Give me strength! Find out, man!'

'Sir, it was Dr Band's secretary who phoned Sergeant Court. She said the doctor had taken the call himself, grabbed his bag and run, shouting to her to send an ambulance to Broadfields and tell the police there'd been another shooting in the woods. That's all she knew.'

'I see.' Suddenly Thorne looked up hopefully. 'Maybe if Band was in such a hurry the shooting wasn't fatal. Perhaps we can learn something.' He pushed his chair back and stood up. 'What are we waiting for? Let's go.'

CHAPTER 18

By the time Dr Band arrived at Broadfields, the initial confusion had subsided. Clare had been carried into the house and was lying on a sofa in the sitting-room. She had just regained consciousness, but was obviously in considerable pain and pale with shock. She was trying to speak, to warn Lorna, whispering Holly's name. Band, busy examining her, told her to be quiet, and her mother bent over her, 'It's all right, darling,' she said. 'John's told us all about it. Everything's under control. Just lie still.'

'I'm going to give you something for the pain, my girl,' Dr Band intervened. 'It'll make you drowsy, and by the time you wake up you'll be in hospital in Oxford.' He busied himself with a hypodermic, and nodded encouragingly at Lorna. 'As far as I can see she should be all right once they've got the bullet out,' he said. 'She was lucky.'

'Lucky?' Lorna smiled wanly. 'I must go with her in the ambulance. But what about Holly?'

'I know,' said Band. 'That's the next problem. Nina's out looking for her with Richard. But I don't like the idea of a panicky child loose with a gun — and nor will the police — '

At first Nina had been incredulous. They had tried to persuade her to await the arrival of the authorities, but even when she accepted John's version of the events, she had scorned their fears for her safety.

'My dears, Holly won't shoot *me*,' she had said. 'I still can't believe she really meant to shoot you either, John, whatever you say. She must have just found the rifle, and you frightened her.'

John Derwent had shrugged. If that was what Nina wanted to think, he didn't care. Personally, he wasn't so sure. Maybe he had scared Holly, but he remembered the look in her eyes, and remained convinced that if Clare hadn't flung him out of the way, he'd almost certainly have been dead or badly wounded. Instead, it was Clare herself . . . If anything happened to Clare . . .

Now he was waiting in the hall for the verdict. Dr Band emerged from the sitting-room with Lorna to reassure him, as a concourse of sirens announced the arrival of the ambulance and Sergeant Court with a constable.

Within a few minutes, Clare, now thoroughly sedated, was loaded into the ambulance, and her mother followed. As Lorna passed John, she put out a hand and squeezed his arm, saying. 'I'll phone as soon as there's any more news, I promise. In the meantime, you stay here and cope with the police. Make them find Holly, but don't let them be too hard on her.' Lorna's gaze was appealing. The ambulance set off and Dr Band, after a brief word with Court, climbed into his own car and went after it.

'Now, sir,' said Sergeant Court, producing his

notebook. 'Just briefly, till the Super arrives.'

To John's annoyance, the Sergeant's reaction to his story was very similar to Nina's. 'Not Miss Holly! It must have been an accident. She'd never do a thing like that on purpose.'

'If you'd been me, looking down the business end of that rifle, you'd be having your doubts about that,' John said acidly.

'But I can't understand it, sir.'

'I can understand it in a way,' John said slowly, 'if she panicked. But why should she panic at the sight of Clare and me? It just doesn't make any kind of sense.'

Sergeant Court made no immediate reply, but went into a mumbled consultation with his constable. John turned away, exasperated. He really wasn't prepared to think about Holly. It was Clare who occupied his mind. He'd have to deal with Court and then Superintendent Thorne, show them the tree, tell them everything in detail, make sure they began a systematic—and sympathetic—search for Holly. Then he himself would be off to Oxford, and the hospital.

Abbot drove flat out, the police siren ripping through the air if any vehicle threatened to impede their progress. Thorne sat beside him, watching the road unwind, silently urging him on. In what seemed a very short time the car was screaming up the drive and sliding to a halt in front of Broadfields.

'Where the hell is everyone?' said Thorne. He reached across Abbot, put his hand on the horn, and kept it there.

Sergeant Court and John Derwent emerged from the woods at a run. When they reached Thorne, John repeated his story, Court added, 'The site's just as he says, sir. I've left a man there.'

'Are you sure it was you the girl intended to shoot?' Thorne demanded.

'I'm sure she aimed at me, yes,' said John. 'If
Clare — Miss Derwent — hadn't pushed me aside, I'd be in
that ambulance right now.'

'We know the child doesn't like you much,' Thorne said
reflectively. 'Remember that outburst of hers in the
church when you arrived unexpectedly at her father's
funeral?'

'Yes,' said John shortly.

'And we also know she can handle a rifle. According to
Mrs Derwent, the whole family used to spend its time
shooting at tin cans and rabbits.' When John was silent,
he continued, 'The only thing is to see what the little girl's
got to say for herself, but to do that we've got to find her.
You say that Mrs Langden and Mr Richard Derwent are
out looking?'

'Yes. Mrs Langden said something about the churchyard.'

'Hm. With the woods as well, it's a big area. And she
could easily be back in the outbuildings, or even in the
house by now. Luckily I've got some reinforcements.' As
he spoke a police van drew up, to disgorge a group of
uniformed officers from Kidlington. 'Abbot,' said the
Superintendent, 'get those men organized. I thought we'd
be having another look for a gun. Well, we are, but this
time it's in the hands of a live child who doesn't seem to
mind using it. So tell them to take care. Don't frighten
her. Don't corner her. If you find her and she won't come
out, fetch me. And if you see Mrs Langden or Mr Richard
Derwent, send them back to the house. We can't have the
whole damned area swarming with amateurs. Someone
might get hurt.' He sounded angry, as if he were relieving
his feelings by taking action — any action. Then he drew
Abbot aside, and murmured, 'And get a good team to go
through the house — it's an ideal chance. Tell them to
keep their eyes skinned. You never know. Apart from the
girl, they might find something of interest, perhaps even

a bright pink shirt or slacks.'

Abbot's eyes narrowed at the unexpected instructions, but he nodded his understanding immediately. 'And if we do find the child holed up in one of the rooms?'

'Just leave her there, and call me. I think we'll try and get Mrs Langden to deal with that sort of situation.'

Thorne beckoned to John Derwent and they strode off together. Almost in silence they reached the woods and found the constable Court had left there wandering rather aimlessly up and down the path. 'Not a sign of anyone since I got here, sir.'

'Right. Come with us.'

John showed them where he and Clare had been standing when they heard the strange noise of something metallic falling, then led the way to the small clearing where they'd found Holly. Thorne gazed up at the tree. No low branches, smooth bark, and at the top thick foliage. It would be a very secret place and, to all appearances, inaccessible. How inaccessible?

The Superintendent looked at the police constable speculatively. 'Any good at climbing?'

The man was startled. 'I couldn't get up that thing, sir. Not without a ladder. Doubt if anyone could.'

Thorne pointed to a neighbouring tree. 'What about up that one and out along that branch?'

The officer looked down at his neat tunic and brightly-polished shoes. 'If you say so, sir.'

'Can't I try it?' John Derwent said, taking pity on the constable.

Thorne eyed him carefully, assessing his weight and reach. 'All right, that might be better. But go slowly. I want to watch you step by step.'

It was a crazy operation, John thought, but he did as he was told, climbing the tree slowly and laboriously. When he reached the branch that led across to what Clare had called the Nest he could see the dilapidated remains of their old tree-house clearly, though they were completely invisible from the ground. 'What now?' he shouted down to Thorne. 'Do you want me to go across?'

'If you can, yes. But take care.'

The distance along the branch was no more than six feet, but as soon as he put his weight on it John knew it wouldn't bear him. There was an alarming creaking, and he hurriedly backed against the trunk.

'I can't make it, Superintendent. I'm surprised Holly could, but I don't suppose she weighs much,' he said. 'Can I come down?'

'Yes. Thank you. As fast as you like.' And when John reached the ground, Thorne said. 'You're an athletic young man, but it was an easy climb, wasn't it?'

'A walk—except for that branch.'

'D'you think it would have been possible to throw the rifle from this tree to the other?'

'Sure. But—' John frowned. 'Why should Holly have done that?'

'If you've just killed someone, Mr Derwent, presumably you want to hide the gun and get out of the wood as quickly as possible. You don't want to waste time crawling across creaking branches.' Thorne was pensive.

'I see that,' said John. 'But what I don't understand is why she didn't leave it there? Why go and recover it? You wouldn't have found it. You hadn't found it, in fact.'

'We might, sometime. Someone might have remembered the tree-house and mentioned it. Or it might have become visible when the leaves fell. Or a gale might have brought it down.' Superintendent Thorne smiled thinly. 'Much better to get the rifle out of harm's way—as far from the woods as possible, somewhere where the chance of it ever being found was really negligible.'

'But why was it so important that it shouldn't be found?'

By now John Derwent and the Superintendent were walking back to the house. The constable had been left to his boredom in the clearing. Thorne stopped in his tracks so that John was forced to stop too.

'Mr Derwent,' Thorne began, his face grim. 'When we find the rifle, as we shall, I expect it to be identified as the one stolen from the Derwents before Christmas. The thief they had in the neighbourhood at the time got the blame, but unjustly I believe. I think the rifle was taken and hidden somewhere — possibly in the woods, but not in the tree-house — until the opportunity to use it arose.'

'But, my God — you're saying Holly deliberately and cold-bloodedly planned to kill her father —'

'No.' Thorne shook his head and started to walk forwards. 'In my opinion Trevor Grayson was always the intended victim. Peter Derwent was mistaken for Grayson because he was wearing his bright yellow slicker.'

'But why —' John Derwent began.

Thorne interrupted him. 'Ah, I see Mr Railton's arrived,' he said.

Tim Railton had been with a client when Richard telephoned before setting out to search for Holly with Nina. He drove up to Broadfields just as the couple returned from their fruitless mission, sent back by the police. Railton was appalled at Richard's story, at the police all over the house and grounds, at Nina's condition, close to tears and breakdown. It was a relief when Superintendent Thorne, obviously in charge, returned with John.

Nodding a greeting to Railton, he said, 'She's not been found yet?'

'No.' Railton was grim. 'Your men say she's not in the house. They're still looking in the outbuildings.'

'No luck at the church either, Mrs Langden?'

Nina shook her head. 'I was sure she'd be somewhere round there. It's her favourite place. But Mr Kent helped us make a thorough search, and your men are still looking. Simon'll stay on watch in case she goes there later.'

'What about the Meakins' farm?' Richard said. 'It's not far away across the fields.'

'We'll try it,' Thorne said at once, gesturing to Sergeant Abbot, who had appeared at his side. 'But if there's no sign of her in the next half-hour I'll have to put out a general call—for her own safety, if nothing else. You agree, Mr Railton?'

'Yes.' Tim Railton overcame a natural reluctance. The idea of the police looking for Holly to help them with their enquiries was somehow repugnant, but it had to be done. 'There's really no option.'

John Derwent had been growing impatient. He said, 'If no one wants me here any more, I'm off to Oxford—to Clare.'

'I'll follow you in my own car,' Railton said at once. 'If that's all right, Superintendent? Mrs Langden and Richard will cope with anything here.'

'That will be fine,' said Thorne. Then, unexpectedly, he added, 'Do your best to reassure Mrs Derwent, Mr Railton. We'll do all we can, and I fully expect Holly to be home before the day's out. We'll have a WPC—a policewoman—waiting for her, and I'll make sure it's one who's also a nurse. I promise we won't take any hasty action.'

Railton and John nodded their thanks, though in the event Superintendent Thorne's optimistic expectations were not to be fulfilled. Many hours were to pass before Holly Derwent was finally found.

CHAPTER 19

There was little sleep at Broadfields that night. Nina went up to her room about one o'clock, but her light remained on. Richard too went to bed eventually, and slept for a few hours. But Lorna insisted on staying up, waiting. She and Tim Railton, who had driven her back from Oxford as soon as it was known that Clare was out of danger, sat together in the sitting-room.

They were constrained and on edge, aware of the policewoman in the kitchen and the patrol around the house. They spoke — when they spoke — desultorily and in low voices. Mostly they sat or paced the room or peered out of the window, drinking innumerable cups of instant coffee prepared by the policewoman. Time passed with agonizing slowness.

Watching Lorna's exhausted face, Railton suddenly said, 'My dear, when all this is over, I'm going to take you away for a long holiday.'

'I don't think it'll ever be over, Tim. It's a continuing nightmare, like one of those TV serials that go on and on, with one crisis following another. Thank God, Clare's going to be all right. But Holly—' Lorna choked. 'Oh, Tim, what's going to happen to Holly? I'm so afraid for her.'

'I don't know, Lorna. I honestly can't tell at this stage. There are too many imponderables,' Railton said slowly. 'First she's got to be found and questioned. But she's only a child, and whatever she's done I promise you nothing dreadful will happen to her.'

Lorna nodded her understanding, and a little later Railton persuaded her to lie on the sofa. He fetched a light rug to cover her, and around dawn she fell into a fitful sleep. For a while he sat watching her, wondering if he would be able to make good on his promise about Holly. Then he went upstairs to take a shower and borrow a razor and a clean shirt from Richard.

The telephone rang as he was coming down. The WPC came out of the kitchen to take the call, but handed him the receiver. 'For you, sir. Mr Kent.'

'Tim? I guessed I'd find you at Broadfields.' Simon Kent sounded excited. 'Tim, I've found the rifle. What shall I do?'

'Holly?' Railton asked at once.

'No. No sign of her. The church is always locked at night because of vandals, but I did look around and in the garden shed. The rifle was in —' he hesitated — 'in the churchyard. She must have been there during the night.'

'I see. Well, you must tell the police, Simon. Immediately. Ring Sergeant Court in Colombury. He'll let Superintendent Thorne know. I'll tell the officers on duty here.'

'Tim! What is it?' The ringing of the phone and Railton's voice had woken Lorna, and she staggered out of the sitting-room into the hall. 'Is it Holly?'

Railton said a quick goodbye to Kent and put down the receiver. 'Not yet, but she can't be far away. And one good thing, Lorna, she's abandoned the rifle. Simon Kent's found it.'

'Oh, thank God! I was so scared, Tim, in case she might — turn it on herself.' Her ultimate fear put into words, Lorna couldn't restrain her tears. She wept uncontrollably.

Between them Railton and the policewoman helped her back to the sofa. There, Railton put his arms around her and held her close. 'It's all right, my darling,' he said quietly, almost to himself. 'It's all right. The rifle's safe, and we'll find Holly soon.'

Superintendent Thorne hadn't had much sleep either. He was convinced that the case had reached a critical point, and he'd only reluctantly called off the search for Holly when darkness fell the previous evening, giving instructions that it should be resumed at first light. Finally, having called the hospital for the latest bulletin on Clare Derwent's condition, he had sent Abbot back home to Kidlington, but had himself decided to stay near at hand. In the end, he spent an uncomfortable night on a makeshift bed in Colombury police station.

Sergeant Court woke him with the news that the rifle had been found. The Superintendent gulped a cup of black tea, washed and dressed hastily and set off with Court for the rectory. Yesterday, he thought, with a third shooting and a child on the run with a murder weapon, had been abysmal. At least today was showing slightly more promise.

They found Simon Kent having breakfast in his kitchen. The rifle, covered with muddy earth, was lying on a piece of newspaper on the draining-board. Thorne regarded it with satisfaction. There was probably little chance of success with fingerprints, but the police had the bullets that had killed Derwent and Grayson and the ballistic experts might well be able to prove they came from this particular weapon. The serial number would show if this was the rifle supposedly stolen from the Derwents.

'How did you come to find it, Mr Kent, and where?'

'I couldn't sleep, so I got up early. I went to the church first. Then I walked round the churchyard.' Kent smiled self-deprecatingly. 'I wanted to assure myself that everything was as it should be. You may not recall, Superintendent, but it's Mr Grayson's funeral today; he's to be buried here this afternoon, It was his express wish, according to his executors, and I was happy there was a plot available.'

'Yes, of course,' said Thorne. 'And the rifle?'

'I was passing Peter Derwent's grave. It's still a mound of earth—you know how they take time to settle—and I noticed it looked untidy. The daisies poor little Holly insists on scattering on it were mostly covered over, and the earth was badly disturbed. I thought of tidying it, and got a spade. I struck metal six inches down. The rifle.'

'Buried with her father.' Sergeant Court shook his head in disbelief.

Thorne was impatient. 'The question is—when? Did you hear any sounds in the night, Mr Kent?'

'I was up till midnight and I'd promised Mrs Langden I'd keep an eye out in case Holly turned up. I don't believe it could have been buried before then, though it wouldn't have been a very noisy business, would it? And I was up at six.'

'So possibly during those six hours,' said Thorne, considering. The wretched child must have been somewhere near while they were searching for her yesterday. He looked around him—Broadfields with its stables and other outbuildings, the damned woods, the old Norman church, the rectory. Suddenly an idea occurred to him. 'Sergeant Court, do you know? Was the rectory ever searched?'

'I don't think so, sir. Not as far as I know,' said Court.

'But I was here,' Simon Kent protested. 'Most of the time,' he added weakly.

'Yes,' said the Superintendent doubtfully. 'But she could have slipped in, you know. She could be in an attic or a cupboard somewhere. Let's go and have a look anyway, sir.'

Holly heard them. She heard the bang of the trapdoor that gave access to the attic, and men's voices. 'You hold the steps and I'll go up.' It was the chief policeman. 'Though how she could have got up here by herself, I can't think.' There were heavy footsteps, then Thorne again. 'Anyway, she's not here. The floor's covered with dust and there are no marks.'

Holly shivered as she heard him clumping about beneath her. She was afraid of Superintendent Thorne, of the way he regarded her speculatively, of the way she could almost see his mind working. She sensed that he'd always distrusted her.

She was glad when she heard the trapdoor bang again, and knew they'd left the loft. Somehow it made her feel a lot safer, which was absurd. They could search the rectory from top to bottom and they'd never find her. They'd never think of looking on the roof.

She'd found this hide-out and the means of getting to it over a year ago. The Kents were away and she'd been wandering round the outside of the rectory, peering in the windows. A rain-water butt, a drainpipe tempted her. It wasn't a difficult climb and she soon found herself on a broad ledge above the window of the dining-room, staring into Mrs Kent's bedroom. A little embarrassed, she'd continued to explore, and discovered that she could easily reach the roof, and a small, secret place between gable and chimney-stack.

Until yesterday she'd not gone there again. But when she'd fled from the woods, terrified that she'd killed Clare, she had instinctively made for home. Then as she broke from the trees she had realized she was still clutching the rifle, and turned aside towards the church. Once she was there, sobbing for breath, half-hysterical, she had known it was no use. It was one of the first places they'd look. So she'd hidden the rifle in the rain-water butt, and climbed on to the rectory roof.

It had been a dreadful night. Luckily there had been no rain, but in shorts and a thin T-shirt she'd been cold, and she'd been hungry. She'd thought of Clare and her father and Trevor Grayson, of Broadfields and the threat to the family. She'd wept till she was sick.

When it was dark, and the rectory lights had gone out, she'd climbed down, recovered the rifle and buried it in her father's grave. She knew about graves. The mound of earth would subside in time, a stone or a monument of some kind would be erected and no one would ever disturb it, she thought. The rifle would lie there for ever, undiscovered.

But now? It was morning again, and there were clouds in the sky and it looked as if it might rain. There was no shelter on the roof. Her hunger had passed, but she was unbearably thirsty. Sooner or later she would have to come down and face her mother and Aunt Nina—and Superintendent Thorne. If only she'd not killed Clare . . . Miserably, biting the end of her thumb, Holly started to cry again.

Thorne, disappointed that his bright idea hadn't paid off and Holly hadn't been found in the rectory, reorganized the search for her. He was happier now that she no longer had the rifle, which was already on its way to the ballistics laboratory, but he knew she must be found as soon as possible, and he couldn't contain his residual fear that finding her might mean another body.

He left Sergeant Court in charge of the search; he was thorough and efficient, and maybe he wouldn't scare the child as much as a stranger might. He himself needed Sergeant Abbot, who had reappeared from Kidlington with the rest of the team.

Together they went to Broadfields. There they found a constable on patrol outside, the policewoman resting in a spare room, Lorna, finally persuaded to lie on her bed in an exhausted sleep, and Nina still upstairs. But in the kitchen Betty Meakin was cheerfully preparing breakfast for Tim Railton and Richard.

'I came over to help out with the stables,' she

explained. 'Richard can't do everything by himself.'

Thorne had been momentarily startled by the sight of the attractive girl in a shocking pink shirt, but he reminded himself that yesterday Abbot had reported similarly coloured garments in Holly's room, and in Clare's and Nina Langden's. As Joe Wilson had pointed out, it was a popular shade, and not restricted to Mrs Kent.

Tim Railton said, 'John Derwent's just phoned from Oxford. Clare had a good night and she's completely out of danger. The bullet missed anything vital, and it's just a matter of healing.'

'That's great,' said Thorne, averting his hungry gaze from the plate of bacon and eggs that Betty Meakin had just placed in front of Richard. 'We'll be off, then. But try not to worry. We're concentrating all our resources on the hunt for Holly. And we'll be back this afternoon for Mr Grayson's funeral.' He smiled to himself as he left with Sergeant Abbot; it was quite clear that no one at Broadfields had remembered that Trevor Grayson was to be buried that day.

From Broadfields, the Superintendent and his sergeant set off for Reading. They stopped en route to allow the Superintendent to have a substantial breakfast. 'Pity we haven't been able to get any sort of line on Williams's past,' said Thorne with his mouth full.

'We're not even sure where he was or what he was doing in Africa,' Abbot observed. 'As far as I can see, few of these African states have any real entry or exit records, and you can get away with anything in a lot of them—especially if there's some sort of war going on. And if Williams was involved in anything illegal—if he was a mercenary or smuggling arms, for instance—the last thing he'd have done was draw attention to himself. But does it really matter, sir?'

'I think so, Sergeant.' Thorne, his breakfast finished, was prepared to be forthcoming. 'I'm convinced that if we're to finish off this case properly we've got to show a connection — some connection we don't yet know about — between Trevor Grayson and Peter Derwent. At first, at least ostensibly, the connection was brother Michael, but he was already dead when Grayson first appeared at Broadfields. I don't believe Peter Derwent would have submitted to this scale of blackmail because of something his black sheep brother had done. So, could the connection be Arthur Williams? I rather suspect it was. Unfortunately suspicion isn't enough.'

'But, sir — ' Abbot hesitated. To him the answer seemed simple. 'What about Holly? Surely she must know why her Dad was being threatened, or else she wouldn't have — '

'Must she? Sure, I guess she knew her father was being blackmailed, but I'd be surprised if she knew why. Would you keep the whole story from your wife, Abbot, yet tell your thirteen-year-old daughter all about it?'

Bill Abbot, who had no wife and couldn't imagine himself in the same circumstances as Peter Derwent, was silent, and Thorne showed no inclination to continue the conversation. They drove on to Reading, and it wasn't until they had reached the outskirts of the town, and had located the hospital that the Superintendent spoke again.

'You've got the pictures?' he asked, as they turned into a drive through grounds that looked as if they could do with the services of an extra gardener or two and drew up in front of a large school-like building.

'Yes, sir. As you know, Peter Derwent's is a fairly good blow-up from that snap his wife gave us, but the best we could do with Grayson was a post mortem photograph; they're never really good likenesses, so it's no wonder that bank manager in London wouldn't swear he was the Reverend Arthur.'

'Can't be helped,' Thorne said. 'Anyway, let's see what

the people here have to say.'

In fact, they had little to say, or at least little to add to what they had said before. All the members of the staff who remembered or had had any contact with Williams were eager to be helpful. But Williams had been lost in a world of his own and Trevor Grayson, his friend, hadn't been communicative.

'At least you can confirm for us that this was the Mr Grayson you knew,' Thorne said at last. He nodded to Abbot, who produced Grayson's photograph. 'It's not a very good likeness, I'm afraid, but it was taken after his death.'

The likeness or otherwise worried no one. Trevor Grayson was instantly and unanimously recognized. 'And he was the only visitor Mr Williams ever had during the whole time he was here?' Thorne asked.

'Yes, the only one.'

Thorne held out his hand to Abbot for the other photograph. 'Now, have you seen this man before?' he asked. 'I accept that he didn't visit Mr Williams, but perhaps he came to your hospital in some other capacity. For instance, he might have driven Mr Grayson here on some occasion. Once more, I'm afraid it's not an ideal portrait—we had to enlarge it from a snapshot.' He passed the photograph of Peter Derwent to the medical officer.

The medical officer glanced at it and frowned. In silence he handed it to the matron, who in turn gave it to the nurse. The three of them stared at Thorne.

Then the medical officer shook his head. 'You must be joking, Superintendent,' he said.

'I assure you I'm not,' Thorne said stiffly.

'But, Superintendent,' the medical officer protested. 'As far as we can tell—and admittedly it's not a good picture—this looks like a photograph of Arthur Williams, our former patient.'

CHAPTER 20

For the second time in a couple of weeks there was an open grave in St Mary's churchyard. For the second time in a couple of weeks the traditional handfuls of earth thudded gently on to a coffin. The Reverend Simon Kent said the final prayers of Trevor Grayson's funeral. The rain was getting heavier, and a few umbrellas blossomed.

On the whole it was a sorry sight, with many fewer people than had met to mourn Peter Derwent. Lorna and Richard had come with Tim Railton. Mrs Wilson was there with her publican brother-in-law. Two groups stood slightly apart: Superintendent Thorne and Sergeant Abbot represented the authorities, and two obviously disinterested young men from Grayson's London Trust Company represented the executors. A few reporters and a photographer had hurried away before the final hymn. There were no relations, seemingly no close friends. The funeral of this murder victim had managed to interest only a score or so of curious onlookers.

The Superintendent had unobtrusively been keeping a close watch about the area, hoping against hope that Holly might be sufficiently attracted by the event to put in an appearance. In spite of his men's failure to find her, he was still sure she wasn't far from home. Suddenly he made up his mind. 'Abbot, as soon as this is over, we'll give them a few minutes, then go along to Broadfields.'

The Rector was shaking hands with the two men from London, who were eager to leave. Other people were drifting away to their cars or, if they'd come on foot, were walking off. Strolling slowly through the churchyard in order to waste a little time, Thorne glanced over his shoulder to say a word to Abbot, who was a pace or two behind him. Immediately he stiffened.

'What is it, sir?'

Thorne drew a deep breath and released it slowly. He seemed to be staring over Abbot's shoulder in the direction of the rectory. Casually he turned away. 'Don't look now, Sergeant. Don't turn around. Keep following me,' he said quietly. 'I've just seen a shadow pass the rectory kitchen window and it could—it could be that damned child. Let's work our way round and have a word with Kent.'

'A difficult service,' Simon Kent said as they approached. 'It was good of you both to come.'

Thorne smiled without warmth. He came to the point at once. 'Mr Kent, should there be anyone in your house at the moment?'

'Why, no.' Kent was mildly surprised. 'Do you want—'

Thorne cut him short. 'This is what I want, sir.'

He explained briefly, and Simon Kent led them around to the rectory garden door. As usual, it had been left open. The two police officers hung back, and let the Rector go into the house ahead of them.

'Hello, Holly,' Simon Kent said.

Holly glanced up, but made no reply. She was sitting at the kitchen table, a glass of milk clutched in her hands, a pathetic sight. Her face was grubby and tear-stained, her clothes torn and indescribably filthy. She had lost the ribbon that usually restrained her hair, and it hung, bedraggled, about her shoulders. She looked unloved, uncared for, a waif. But it was her eyes that horrified the parson. They were slightly unfocused and desperate, without hope. He had seen down-and-outs sleeping rough in London who bore just the same expression.

In three strides he was around the table, had knelt beside Holly and gathered her into his arms. His words came tumbling out, intended to reassure. 'My dear child, thank God you're here. You're safe. That's wonderful.

We've all been so worried about you — your mother and Aunt Nina and Richard and Clare. We — '

'No, that's not true.' Holly's voice was shrill as she tried to push him away from her. 'Clare's dead. I shot her. I killed her.'

'Holly, you didn't kill her. Listen to me!' Kent shook the small girl in his determination to make her understand. 'Clare's fine. You wounded her and she's in hospital, but she'll soon be well and home again. She knows it was an accident. You didn't mean to hurt her, did you?'

'No, I didn't, Mr Kent! I didn't! I meant — '

'Then that's splendid, and everything's going to be all right. I'll take you home now. We'll go in my car. Come along, Holly dear.'

Standing in the passage outside the kitchen door, Thorne cursed under his breath. If the Rector hadn't interrupted at the crucial moment, the child might have said something useful. 'I meant — ' What had she meant? But the chance was gone now for the moment. He could hear Kent and the girl moving, and he signalled Abbot to go out the way they had come, through the garden door.

Outside, he said at once, 'Broadfields, Abbot. You get the car and bring it round there — and call off the search. I'll cut straight across the fields and be there before the girl. I'll warn them Holly's coming, make sure the WPC's ready for her, and send for Dr Band. I don't want all the family questioning her immediately. Get going.'

'Yes, sir,' said Abbot, and wondered why the Superintendent was bending the regulations in Holly Derwent's favour. Surely it wasn't right to let her go off alone like this with the parson. Suppose she tricked him and escaped again? She might only be a child, but she was a bloody menace; she'd already proved that. Sergeant Abbot was glad it wasn't his responsibility. 'Yes, sir,' he said again as he started for the car.

*

Three-quarters of an hour later Superintendent Thorne was reasonably satisfied; he had achieved all his main objectives. Holly was safely in her own bed. She was clean and warm and fed and, thanks to the sedative Band had given her, fast asleep. Lorna had been persuaded to leave her, but the policewoman was in the room. The doctor, in a hurry to get to another patient, had left, and so had the parson, though reluctantly. Almost by instinct the household—Lorna, Richard and Nina Langden—had assembled in the sitting-room, with Tim Railton.

Fingering his moustache, Thorne smiled at them all with seeming benevolence. He had a definite purpose in mind and, if at all possible, he intended to achieve it. He glanced at Abbot, seated discreetly towards the back of the room, and cleared his throat.

Before he could speak, the door opened and John Derwent walked in.

'Holly?' he asked at once.

'She's all right,' said Lorna. 'She's upstairs asleep in bed. And Clare?'

'She's fine. They hope to let her out by the end of the week. I've just come over to collect some clothes. Then I'm going back to Oxford—'

Thorne had been watching these exchanges with ill-concealed impatience. Now he interrupted. 'As you're here, you might as well stay for a while, Mr Derwent. I was just going to have a word with the immediate family, and I gather you're likely to be part of it soon.' The Superintendent cleared his throat again and glanced around the group.

'First of all, I'm just as relieved as you are that Holly's been found, alive and in reasonably good shape. But I'm sure you appreciate that she presents a problem. Two people have been killed and another wounded. Admittedly Holly's only just in her teens, and we don't treat children like adults in this country. Nevertheless—'

'Wait a minute, Superintendent!' Railton said quickly. 'You're going much too fast, jumping to conclusions. Obviously there's no question that Holly shot and wounded her sister. She'd just found the murder weapon—or what she thought was the murder weapon, the rifle that had killed her father. She was holding it, and she panicked. But that's no reason to suppose she had anything to do with the two killings.'

'Isn't it, sir?' Thorne was no longer trying to give any appearance of benevolence. 'What makes you say she'd just *found* the rifle? What made her suddenly decide to climb up to that disused tree-house? Why was she caught near the same spot by one of my men when the woods were supposed to be closed to the public? What's more, why did she actually bite him when he tried to restrain her? More panic? Anyway, if she'd just found the rifle when John and Clare saw her, why should she panic at all? It would have been more natural for her to be pleased with herself for being cleverer than the police. Triumph perhaps—yes. But panic—no! And lastly, after she'd run away, why did she go so far as to bury the gun in her father's grave?'

George Thorne paused for breath. No one said anything. He looked from one more or less shocked face to the next, and wished he could know what each was thinking. Even Sergeant Abbot was looking a little shaken by his outburst. He'd have to be careful now, Thorne thought. One false move, and he could achieve nothing. And if he achieved nothings, his methods might well be considered questionable. He smiled grimly.

'It was extremely important that the rifle shouldn't be found,' he continued, adopting a milder tone. 'Unless I'm badly mistaken it'll turn out to be the one that was stolen from here before last Christmas. Maybe it was originally taken on some sort of impulse. But it was kept, cared for and later hidden in a strategic place in the woods until the right opportunity presented itself. In other words, the killing was premeditated.'

There was a chorus of expostulation, and Lorna shook her head violently. 'No! No, I don't believe it,' she said. 'Not Holly. She loved her father dearly. Why on earth should she suddenly decide to kill —'

Overcome by distress, Lorna buried her face in her hands. Railton put his arm around her and glared at Thorne. 'Superintendent, I don't know what you're trying to get at, but surely it's not necessary to upset Mrs Derwent in this fashion. Really, I protest.'

'I'm sorry,' Thorne said. 'But just bear with me for a few more minutes. Believe me, it's important.'

'Why?' Richard was aggressive. 'Mum's right. Holly would never have killed Dad.'

'As I see it, Mr Derwent was killed by accident,' Thorne said. 'He was visiting Mr Grayson when the storm broke. According to the housekeeper, Mrs Wilson, he insisted on leaving, but borrowed an old yellow slicker of Mr Grayson's. He seems to have set off through the woods, but something made him change his mind — perhaps a falling tree, perhaps a particularly loud clap of thunder — and he turned to retrace his steps to the road. He was shot in the back.'

His audience's reaction was immediate. Thorne waited until the barrage of questions had died down, and then said, 'Mr Railton, you asked me what evidence I have. You know perfectly well I'm not obliged to reveal my evidence at this stage, but I'm prepared to take the argument a little further, if you'll permit me.' Then, turning to Lorna, who had by now regained her composure, he spoke as if addressing her alone. 'Mrs Derwent, no one has been able to produce any reason whatsoever why your husband should have been killed. But he was wearing Mr Grayson's distinctive oilskins, and it was pouring with rain. Visibility was limited, and anyone seeing him emerge from Grayson's cottage could very well have assumed that he was Grayson. Indeed, a lady in one of the council houses on the other side of the road, a Mrs Daley, did just that.'

'You mean someone was watching and actually saw Peter leave the cottage?' Nina Langden said.

'In fact, we think more than one person saw him at about that time, Mrs Langden,' Thorne said. 'After all, it must have taken a few minutes to run and get the rifle and be ready to shoot — Trevor Grayson — if he decided to come through the woods.'

There was a moment's silence at this, and John Derwent said, 'Go on, Superintendent, tell us. Why should Holly — or anyone else — plan to kill Grayson?'

'Blackmail is often a hazardous occupation, Mr Derwent,' Thorne said slowly. 'Possibly one of the most hazardous crimes, especially as there's usually a good deal of sympathy for anyone who decides to take it upon him or herself to rid the world of a blackmailer. Nevertheless—'

'Blackmailer?' Richard interrupted, as if the full implications of what the Superintendent had been saying had just sunk in. 'Trevor Grayson — a blackmailer?'

'You mean it was Grayson who was blackmailing Peter, Superintendent?' Railton was incredulous. 'And Grayson was the man who posed as Arthur William Derwent?'

Thorne nodded, as Lorna said, 'But — that's unbelievable. The very day Trevor was shot he was here, and he as good as offered us financial help. I thought it was so kind of him. And — and he left Richard his cottage!'

'There's no doubt, I'm afraid,' said the Superintendent. 'As for the cottage, maybe Grayson thought the Derwent family deserved a little recompense when he was dead and gone. Maybe it was his idea of a joke. We'll probably never know.'

'Wait a minute!' Again Richard interrupted. He looked

accusingly from his mother to Tim Railton. 'Dad was being blackmailed—and you knew about it?'

'Not until after his death,' Railton said. 'And we still don't know why. Do you, Superintendent?'

'Yes, sir. I've a pretty good idea.' Thorne paused, his eyes flicking from one member of the group to another. He said quietly. 'I was rather hoping Mrs Langden would explain more fully.'

Lorna gasped. Richard caught his breath and began to cough. A whisper of disbelief spread around the room. Only Nina Langden showed no real emotion. The knuckles of her clasped hands shone white, but otherwise she was calm, even unnaturally calm, Thorne thought.

'What makes you think I know, Superintendent?'

'Mrs Langden, Holly didn't plot to kill Trevor Grayson. She's only a child, and this was a carefully-planned fully premeditated murder. Besides, how would she have known anything about the blackmail? Did she read some letter? Overhear a telephone conversation?' Thorne didn't miss the glance that passed between Tim Railton and Richard at this point and interpreted it correctly. 'Yes,' he said. 'I know. She liked to eavesdrop. She's a curious, enquiring child. But Peter Derwent wasn't a careless man. He wouldn't have given anything away by accident.

'No, Mrs Langden, no one knew about Grayson and Arthur Williams and the blackmail—nobody but the one person in whom Peter Derwent confided—you. And you alone decided to kill Grayson, Mrs Langden.'

For a moment or two there was no reaction. Then Nina Langden laughed, a harsh jarring laugh without any humour. 'Yes, Superintendent,' she said. 'You're perfectly right. I killed Trevor Grayson, and I don't regret it. He deserved to die. If I had to do it again, I would.'

CHAPTER 21

Tim Railton was on his feet, protesting, all his legal instincts aroused. The police had no right to interrogate like this, to accuse on the basis of such meagre evidence, to extract a so-called confession under duress. There had been no charge, no formal warning. Superintendent Thorne was way out of line.

It was Nina herself who waved aside his protests. 'My dear Tim,' she said. 'It doesn't matter any more. I spent a large part of the night writing out a full and free confession, and the Superintendent's welcome to it. I no longer care.'

In the small silence that followed this statement, George Thorne collected himself. He used the time-honoured phrases to warn Nina of her rights. Then he waited.

But Nina, though she acknowledged his warning, was following her own train of thought. 'Why should I care? Why should I? I loved two people more than any others in this world — Michael and Peter. The first was lost to me years ago, and I killed the second. The Superintendent's got it right. It happened just as he said. I'd been for a walk and when the storm broke I was at the far end of the woods by the road near Grayson's cottage. With all that thunder and lightning about I thought I'd better not go back through the trees, but it was pouring hard and I hadn't got a raincoat, so I hesitated. Then I saw someone I took to be Grayson come out of his house. I knew he'd been upping his demands, and I knew Peter was terribly worried about meeting them. It was a chance I couldn't miss. The storm, the noise —'

'The rifle was already in the wood, of course,' Thorne prompted.

'Oh yes. It had been there for months, in a hollow tree, loaded and ready. If you ask me why I put it there I can only say I always knew I'd have to kill him some day, some time.' Nina gave a twisted smile. 'I suppose I hoped that when I did it, it'd be taken for a tragic accident on the part of someone who'd panicked and run away. What I didn't realize was how overcome I'd be when the moment came.' Nina paused, reliving the past. 'I stood there like an idiot, staring at what I thought was Grayson's body, feeling—nothing. Nothing at all; I didn't even try to make sure he was dead. Then I heard a motor-cycle. I ran back to the tree, wrapped up the gun again, hid it and took to my heels. But I was dreadfully slow. Did the motor-cyclist see me?'

'He saw someone in pink running among the trees,' Thorne said, and thought of Jean Kent, and Holly's lie incriminating her.

Nina nodded. 'By the time I got home I was wet through and coughing badly. Lorna saw me and made me go straight to bed. I'd had a cold for days, and she was afraid I'd get 'flu or something.'

Thorne's expression was sardonic. Lorna's unintentional deception, telling him that Mrs Langden was ill in bed, had originally misled him. He said, 'And then you discovered you'd killed Peter, and not Trevor Grayson. That must have been a shock, Mrs Langden.'

Nina Langden reacted immediately. She glared at Thorne. 'If you can call it a mere shock, you've no imagination, Superintendent. Not only had I lost my beloved Peter, but I'd also lost Broadfields, though I didn't know that at the time. Peter never told me of this absurd arrangement he'd made with his American cousin to meet Grayson's demands. I suppose he didn't dare, or perhaps he thought it would grieve me too much to know we'd have to give up Broadfields eventually.'

For a moment Nina Langden lapsed into thought. The silence was almost tangible. The dialogue had been between her and Thorne. No one had interrupted them, and no one now seemed prepared to volunteer a remark.

'Grayson?' Thorne said finally.

'Yes, Grayson,' Nina said. 'Naturally he still had to die. After all, he'd been responsible for everything. For blackmailing Peter and nearly ruining the family, and now, after Peter's—death—for our loss of Broadfields. And the last straw was when he came here that morning with his smarmy offers to buy Clare's mare and help us financially. I just left him to Lorna and went to wait for him in the woods. After I'd shot him I threw the rifle up into the Nest where I hoped it would be safer. I was lucky you'd not found it before in the hollow tree. But I was in a hurry. I knew I had to get back to the kitchen garden and establish my alibi, and it was a poor throw. I meant to go back later with a long stick or something, and make sure it was properly hidden, but there was no chance. The police were everywhere. Then I went and burnt my hand, and I had to ask Holly to help me.'

'How on earth dared you do that?' Lorna demanded. 'How could you involve Holly, Nina?'

Nina regarded Lorna sadly. 'She was already involved. She was in the woods at the time. She heard the shot and she saw me with the rifle. I took her to the kitchen garden with me and told her I'd killed Grayson. I said I'd done it because he'd killed Peter, which was the truth—except that blackmail's worse than a clean bullet.'

'You were using Holly to save yourself,' Lorna said angrily. 'There's no excuse—'

'Please!' Thorne held up a minatory hand. 'Mrs Langden, I'm sure you were going to tell us why Grayson was able to blackmail Peter Derwent. It concerns Michael, doesn't it? It's not Michael's body in that grave in St Mary's churchyard.'

Lorna gasped as Sergeant Abbot looked up sharply. Trust the Superintendent to keep something up his sleeve, he thought. John and Richard exchanged glances. Nina wiped the back of her hand across her brow. 'Could I have a glass of water?' she asked in a voice that was a little tremulous.

Richard went to get it and Thorne, afraid she might be about to collapse under the strain, sent Abbot to fetch the WPC from Holly's room. He was reluctant to interrupt the proceedings by sending for more help, in case he broke the flow of Nina's words. But after two sips of water she seemed to recover herself, and continued calmly enough.

'I loved Michael, but there's no gainsaying he was wild. He and Grayson met as mercenaries—mercenary soldiers—in Africa, fighting for I don't know who. While they were on leave somewhere Michael killed someone. It was over a woman, I think—nothing to do with the war—and he was wanted for murder. With Grayson's help, he managed to get away, back to their unit. Then, not long after, during a battle in the bush, a man called Arthur Williams was killed. He wasn't unlike Michael in appearance, and as insurance in case the murder charge ever caught up with him, Michael took on his identity. I never really understood the details, but I suppose it was easy to do in some uncivilized part of Africa, and I doubt if the mercenary fighters' records were very accurate. Anyway, again with Grayson's help, Michael managed it. He became Arthur Williams, and the body of the real Williams was sent back to England and buried here at St Mary's, just as you say, Superintendent.'

'But what did you mean when you said Michael was lost to you years ago?' asked Railton quickly. 'If he's still alive—'

Nina looked across at Thorne. 'I'm coming to that. I think the Superintendent knows most of the story, or guesses it. I meant what I said. Michael wasn't dead, but he was lost to me forever. It was like this. Grayson's contract was completed and he came back to England. He visited Colombury—do you remember when we first met him, Lorna, just after Gerald's death? The will was about to be probated, and Peter was glad to talk to any friend of his brother about the family circumstances. None of it was secret. Gerald's will left Broadfields to Michael, and to Peter only if Michael died first. It should have been changed when Peter came back to live here permanently, but Gerald never got around to it. Then when we knew that Michael was dead, it no longer mattered; Peter would inherit automatically.'

She paused and drank two more sips from her glass. 'Grayson saw his opportunity,' she went on rapidly. 'He told Peter bluntly that he knew Michael was still alive, but was prepared to keep quiet about it—for a consideration. He didn't ask a lot at that point, I believe.'

'Only what Peter could get for his insurance policies, I expect,' said Railton. 'But all this was before the will was probated. Peter knew his brother was alive and did nothing? He connived at fraud, in effect.'

'Exactly. So he was completely in Grayson's clutches. But he had no choice, did he? He'd given up his army career and was doing his best to keep Broadfields going. He had a wife and three children, and very little money. All he'd got was Broadfields. And now it looked as if he might not even have that. Yes, he had to come to an—an arrangement with Grayson.'

'You mean, he conspired with Grayson and started paying blackmail as a result,' said Richard brutally. 'But how the hell was he sure that Michael wouldn't turn up at any moment?'

'Because Michael was still wanted for that murder in Africa. The situation there was apparently sorting itself out by then, and there was a fair chance the authorities

could successfully have applied for extradition if Michael
ever revealed himself, even here in England. At least,
that's what Grayson persuaded Peter.'

'So Peter thought he was safe,' said Railton. 'Safe—as
long as Grayson kept quiet. But what I don't understand
is why Peter should have believed Grayson in the first
place. What proof could Grayson offer?'

'That's just what I asked Peter myself,' said Nina. 'It
seems that Grayson threatened to go to the police and
have Williams's body exhumed, and force Peter to face
all the scandal and mess that would go with something
like that. And then, when he made his big demands on
Peter, he was in a position to prove his point conclusively.'

'How?'

'A few months after all this, Michael, still in Africa,
was involved in another fight. He got hit on the head and
lost his memory; he became almost like a child. There was
nothing they could do for him out there, so they sent him
home. The only sort of next of kin name they had for him
was Grayson's, and Grayson met him and looked after
him. Eventually he went into a—a kind of mental
hospital in Reading. Still as Williams, of course.' She
stopped speaking and a tear formed in her eye. 'That's
partly what I meant when I said he was lost to me
forever.' Then she shook her head fiercely. 'Anyway,
Grayson was able to take Peter to see Michael—not to
speak to, but to see him walk by in the garden of the
home. There was no doubt it was Michael. Peter told me
all about it. I wanted to go too, but Peter refused to let me.
He said Grayson must never know he'd confided in me.'

'So Dad just had to go on paying,' said Richard. 'But
Michael could never have inherited the estate in his
condition. Any court would have granted the estate to
Dad, with the proviso that he looked after his brother.
Isn't that so, Tim?'

'Yes, probably,' said Railton slowly. 'But it wouldn't

affect the case against Peter for conspiracy and fraud. Though whether the DPP would ever have sanctioned a prosecution in such circumstances, I'm not sure. Why on earth didn't Peter seek proper advice?'

Lorna had been almost silent so far. Now she intervened. 'Perhaps he loved Broadfields too much to risk it,' she said, 'or the Derwent name or the family — or even me — ' She shrugged resignedly.

'Anyway,' concluded Nina, 'rightly or wrongly, that's the story. It's all out in the open. What happens now, Superintendent?'

'Not quite,' said Thorne. 'The story's not quite finished. What none of you know is that Michael Derwent really did die — as Williams, of course — a year or more after Peter Derwent saw him at the hospital. Suddenly one night he had a brain haemorrhage. Grayson never told Peter that — not that it would have made much difference. Peter Derwent's original mistakes — crimes — would still have been outstanding.'

Nina sighed. Her tale told, she looked old and tired and hopeless. She raised her head. 'I repeat, I'm glad I killed Grayson. And I repeat, what happens now, Superintendent?'

'I have to ask you to accompany me to the station, Mrs Langden, where you'll be formally charged with the murder of Trevor Grayson. You may ask for a solicitor, of course — '

'I'll follow you there, Nina,' Tim Railton said at once. 'We'll do everything we possibly can, I assure you.'

'Thanks.' Nina had once again recovered herself, and her expression was sardonic. Pushing herself from her chair, she got to her feet. Momentarily she staggered and John Derwent put out a hand to steady her. She looked down at the shirt and old jeans she was wearing, the scuffed sandals. 'Am I allowed to put on some more respectable clothes before I go, Superintendent?'

Thorne hesitated briefly. 'Yes, all right, Mrs Langden,' he said. He nodded at the woman police constable, then at Abbot. 'You go with them too, Sergeant. Mrs Langden mentioned a written confession.'

'Taking every precaution, I see, Superintendent. Don't worry,' Nina said. 'I don't intend to run away.'

'It's regulations, Mrs Langden,' Thorne began, but without a backward glance, head down, shoulders bowed, her face set in grim lines, Nina Langden had walked from the room, accompanied by the two officers. There was silence till the door shut behind them.

Then Richard said, 'What will happen to her?'

'And to Holly, Superintendent?' Lorna asked.

Thorne smiled wryly. 'We shan't prosecute Holly, Mrs Derwent. If Mrs Langden's confession is accepted, I doubt if the child will even be called as a witness. I'd suggest sending her away from here — away from Broadfields — for a while, so that she can forget about the whole affair!'

'She could come to the States,' John said. 'She could stay with my sister and her family. It would be a real change, and she wouldn't be lonely with Clare nearby.'

'That's very generous of you, John,' Lorna said gratefully.

'But what about Aunt Nina?' Richard persisted.

Thorne shrugged, and Railton replied for him. 'There's not much that can be done really. A good barrister. Diminished responsibility, perhaps. We'll have to wait and see. A lot will depend on the Judge.'

Again they lapsed into silence, considering the implications of Railton's words. Superintendent Thorne was thinking that if only old Gerald had made a new will naming Peter as heir, there would have been no motive for blackmail, no cause for any killings, intentional or not. Idly he wondered if Peter's last words had in fact referred to Gerald's will and to himself, the younger son.

Then from upstairs came a burst of angry noise. A cry of pain, a door slamming, shouting. Thorne was on his feet and running. The others streamed behind him. It wasn't hard to trace the source of the noise. Abbot and the WPC were pounding on the door of Nina's bedroom, shouting at Nina to open it.

'Break it down,' Thorne ordered as he reached them.

The uniformed girl stood aside to let Abbot take a run. 'I'm sorry, sir,' she said. 'It was my fault. As she went into the room the old lady stepped back on my instep hard enough to make me scream with pain. She slammed the door in my face. I just wasn't expecting it.'

Thorne looked at her in disgust, and there was a thud as Abbot hit the door with his shoulder. It shuddered but didn't give. He tried again, again without success.

'Here, let me help,' John Derwent said.

Together he and Abbot had two more runs at the door. At the third try the lock gave and they stood on the threshold. Thorne, swearing under his breath, pushed past them and stared, horrified.

Nina lay on her back, on her bed, blood all around her, an old-fashioned cut-throat razor clenched in her right hand, her throat gaping.

There was a sob behind him. 'It was one of her husband's,' Lorna said inconsequentially. 'He had a full set, one for each day of the week. She kept them as a kind of memento —'

Then the full terror of the moment seized her and she turned, sobbing, into Tim Railton's waiting arms. 'Another death!' Her voice trailed briefly.

Thorne and Railton stared at each other across Lorna's head, and Railton echoed Thorne's unstated thoughts. 'Maybe it was for the best,' he said. 'Maybe —'